A
Holiday Promise

Bernadette Piper

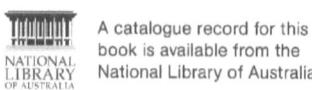
A catalogue record for this book is available from the National Library of Australia

Linellen Press
265 Boomerang Road
Oldbury, Western Australia
www.linellenpress.com.au

Dedication

For Brian, Laura and Anthony.

Acknowledgements

Many thanks to Helen Iles for her editing, support and publishing. Also, Michelle Harris for her positive critique. Thank you to my wonderful peers from the Rockingham Writers Circle, especially Jean, Georgia and Nada. And to my husband Barry, who still holds my hand when we walk.

Contents

Dedication iii

Acknowledgements v

Contents vii

Prologue..1

Chapter One...4

Chapter Two 11

Chapter Three 20

Chapter Four...27

Chapter Five...30

Chapter Six..33

Chapter Seven..38

Chapter Eight..43

Chapter Nine...50

Chapter Ten 57

Chapter Eleven 60

Chapter Twelve 66

Chapter Thirteen 71

Chapter Fourteen 74

Chapter Fifteen..77

Chapter Sixteen..83

Chapter Seventeen 87

Chapter Eighteen 91

Chapter Nineteen 97

Chapter Twenty...100

Chapter Twenty-one..104

Chapter Twenty-two..108

Chapter Twenty-three 112

Chapter Twenty-four...127

Chapter Twenty-five..132

Chapter Twenty-six...136

Chapter Twenty-seven 144

Chapter Twenty-eight..147

Chapter Twenty-nine...150

Chapter Thirty 155

Chapter Thirty-one 160

Chapter Thirty-two 167

Chapter Thirty-three..174

Chapter Thirty-four 178

Chapter Thirty-five 180

Chapter Thirty-six...187

Chapter Thirty-Seven 189

Chapter Thirty-eight..197

Chapter Thirty-nine 203

Chapter Forty 210

Chapter Forty-one 214

Epilogue 220

About the Author 222

Prologue

1978

Light came through stained-glass windows sending colours splashing across the stone floor. He shuffled his feet, then stamped them against the cold and pulled his black cloak tight around his aching shoulders. Quivering fingers struck the match to light the candles; some days, there seemed to be so many.

Cold air wrapped around him; he turned to the chill and glimpsed a silhouette shrouded in mist at the open door. As the haze warmed by the rising sun swirled around, he squinted to get a better look.

She hesitated, her hand on the door. Perhaps she thought she was alone. He hobbled down the aisle, but the girl turned to leave.

'Don't go,' he called. 'Come in out of the cold.'

'No, I ...' She fidgeted, leaning against the door.

Gold and grey fingers of fog floated into the warming sky before vanishing as the sun moved higher, a relief from the cold night.

He could see her now. A halo of golden curls, tangled and unkempt, reflected the early morning sunshine. Her blue school blazer was ripped, her dirty face stained with tears; torn stockings, and her bare feet were splattered with blood. She wrung her hands together as her eyes darted around the building.

He reached out, but she backed away like a frightened animal, so he lowered his hands and said, 'Come inside, it's warmer.'

The girl peered through the dark and gloomy shadows as if ensuring they were alone.

'There is no one else here,' he said.

She stumbled through the doorway, her body shaking, so he removed his cloak and wrapped it over her shoulders, taking care not to touch her.

'Let's sit here.' He directed her to a pew and sat beside her, giving her space. 'Will you tell me your name?'

She shook her head, and tears fell. She was very young, no more than fourteen or fifteen, and if she was who he thought, she'd been missing for nearly a week.

'Are you hungry?'

The girl nodded.

'Shall we go into the house?'

She glanced around the building, shivered, and nodded.

Inside his home, he passed his surprised housekeeper as he guided the girl down the hallway to the kitchen. Sitting her on a chair at the old wooden kitchen table, he took his cloak from her and offered her the blanket, kept for cold nights, from the back of his chair. She dragged it around her shoulders, pulled it under her chin, and clutched it with both hands.

After stirring the logs in the wood stove, he turned on the electric kettle; when the water boiled, he poured tea for himself and made Milo for her. All the time, she sat silently watching his every move.

He sat opposite her and waited. She ate the food he put in front of her slowly, making it last.

'He's dead,' she finally said. 'I killed him.'

Surely, that was not possible; she was no more than a child. He wanted to reach out and comfort her, but it was too soon for that. 'Tell me what happened.'

Tears fell, and her words faltered as she stared at the flames in the stove. 'I told him no, I told him, but he wouldn't listen.'

'What happened?'

'I didn't mean to. It was cold and dark, and I was scared.' The contents of the cup she held spilt over the rim. She placed it on the table and wiped her hands on her dirty dress, blinking her tear-filled eyes. She took a deep breath. 'I let him hold me. He was warm … But he wouldn't stop, I said no, – he wouldn't stop.' Her words faded away, and she looked into his eyes, but he doubted she was seeing him.

'I pushed him. I tried to get up the embankment, but he – I pushed him – he fell, hit his head on the rocks – fell into the river – the tide – I didn't mean to.' She gulped air, her chest heaving. 'I said no.' The girl choked back her tears and bowed her head.

He reached across the table, his hand close to hers. 'You didn't do anything wrong.' She did not pull away.

The sound of the kitchen door opening startled her, and she cried out when she saw his housekeeper standing in the opening, a police officer on either side.

The girl jumped up and scrambled around the table, throwing herself onto the floor beside his chair; she clung to his arm. 'Don't let them take me, don't let them take me.'

He caressed her damp red curls and held her hand firmly.

'I won't let them take you,' Father Francis Kelly promised.

Chapter One

Cara

Cara stumbled down the steps of the tour bus, blinking and gawking at her surroundings – blue sky, snow-covered ground, clean, fresh air. Breathing deeply, she filled her lungs. Like a child, Cara bent and scrunched a handful of snow into a ball. She raised her arm as her friends made their way to the baggage compartment of the white bus with blue lettering on the side.

'Don't you dare?' a voice admonished.

Cara tossed the snowball away but should have looked before doing so. A male voice said, 'Ouch.'

Sunlight bounced off flecks of blond in brown curls as he strode towards her, his hands full of snow, a teasing smile on his face.

Cara's knees turned to jelly. 'Sorry. I'm sorry…' She put her hands over her head in mock fear, and it was mock. That smile sent tingles down her spine.

He let the snowball drop to the ground as he looked down at her, his hand over his heart where a patch of wetness showed. 'Not a problem, I think I'll live.' He hesitated. Cara shuddered.

He pushed his sunglasses onto his head, and Cara's heart missed a beat when their eyes met. His dark golden-brown eyes, warm and intense, brought the gold-splashed muddy soil where she'd picked wild lilies as a child racing into her mind.

'Have you just arrived?' he asked. 'Sorry, of course, you've just arrived….' He looked at the bus, his words fading.

Cara nodded. 'Yes, we just got here.'

'Cara, come and get your bag,' that voice called from the emptying bus. She swung around and answered, 'I'm coming.'

Cara turned back to the man before her. Wild lilies – one of a handful of happy childhood memories etched in her mind. She dragged her gaze away from his. 'I have to go.'

'Okay.'

Cara fled.

**

Tugging her backpack over her shoulder, Cara didn't know which way to look; she was in a Christmas card. Sunshine reflected off snow-covered mountains that soared into the pale blue sky; skiers swished past; any minute now she expected to see Rudolf and the reindeer fly by.

Stepping around puddles and melting snow in the car park, she thought her boots, suitable for winter in Perth, Western Australia, were not going to be good enough for winter in Austria. Cold seeped through the leather as she plodded up the path with the tour group.

The Pension Frieden looked like a picture postcard, with white walls, empty flower boxes in shuttered windows, and a roof and wooden eaves peppered with snow.

The remnants of a snowman distracted her as she reached the front steps of the Pension, and she slipped, landing awkwardly on her haunches. Pushing herself up, she lost her footing on the glassy step and stumbled. Strong hands caught her and helped her stay upright.

'Okay?' a male voice asked. Cara stared into sapphire-blue eyes.

'I'm okay.'

'Sure?'

'Are you alright?' Another voice. Those brown eyes again. She hadn't thought about wild lilies for such a long time.

'Yes, I think so.' Cara glanced at the ground, at the sky, anywhere except into those gold-brown eyes as she dusted the snow from her jeans.

'Caz, are you alright?'

Cara glanced over the shoulder of the man who'd stopped her fall to the girls who stood next to the bottom step, concern on their faces.

'I'm okay, Shaz,' she called out.

'You sure you are okay?' the man supporting her asked. Tall and handsome with light brown hair, he seemed familiar, someone she should know, but he wasn't.

'Yes, thank you,' she said.

Cara steadied her feet on a surface that was more slippery than she expected. Clutching his hand, she bent and hoisted her backpack onto her shoulder then straightened up, still holding his hand. Her eyes wandered to the man beside him, and she hoped her warm face didn't show.

The tour group gathered at the bottom of the step. Quiet, after a long bus trip, they began to find their voices. Cara released the hand she held and stepped aside to allow the tour group to pass. They tramped across the carpeted foyer to the wooden reception desk of the Pension.

'All good?' the blue-eyed man asked.

'Yep.' Cara nodded.

Inside, Cara stood with her friends in the foyer and watched the two men make their way across the room to the reception desk, where they negotiated the crowd with practised skill. The blue-eyed man lounged against the desk and grinned at her. Cara giggled and returned his smile easily; his cheeky smile warming her heart. But the man she'd hit with the snowball, the one with dark eyes, stared over his shoulder at her. She caught her breath, heat prickling her skin, and wild lilies danced in her mind.

What am I doing? This is silly; the fall must have disturbed me more than I thought.

'They're cute. Who are they?' Sharon asked.

'I don't know,' she replied.

'Are they American?'

'I think so.' Indeed, the blue-eyed man might be, but the other man's accent had shades of something else – he didn't sound like the voices in the movies.

'You're useless, Caz.' Sharon gaped at the men at the reception desk. 'Do you think they're staying here?'

Cara shook her head and shrugged her shoulders. Sharon, Cara's friend, always acted like this, and they had shared so much as children. At 5'9", she was five inches taller than Cara, her height emphasising her slim build. With golden-brown skin, amber almost cat-like eyes, and long dark blonde hair, she'd caught the attention of one of Perth's premium modelling agencies. She'd had many relationships, some good, some not so good, and she looked for romance and adventure everywhere she went.

Elizabeth was the other member of their little friendship group; her hazel eyes complimented her dark chin-length bob. She was not as tall as Sharon, but taller than Cara. Elizabeth was a gentle soul and didn't need to know anything more than she loved Cara, and she would always be her friend; that was all any girl needed: two true friends.

The three girls had started talking about this trip before they left high school. Eventually, Elizabeth finished her studies, and they all saved enough money. A working holiday in London, having a white Christmas, then travelling to the snowfields of Austria to learn how to ski, their Contiki Tour a safe way to travel.

Sharon was hopeful of advancing her modelling career, and she'd had some success with a photographer she had met in

London, so her normal behaviour shouldn't bother Cara. The bus trip from London to Gastig, Austria, had been long, maybe she just felt tired.

Cara shook herself. 'I don't know, Shar.' She shifted the backpack on her shoulder and smiled at her friend. 'Come on, let's get a room before all the good ones are gone.'

***

Upstairs, Cara stood looking out the window; the view over snow-covered mountains that stretched into the blue sky seemed unreal. Even though the cold outside was refreshing, Cara was glad to be inside the heated room.

Things hadn't turned out as she'd hoped – the two weeks she'd spent in Dublin before joining her friends in London hadn't changed anything. Dublin, a city in the land of Shamrocks and Leprechauns, a city celebrating its one-thousandth anniversary, had kept its secrets hidden. And Cara kept all her secrets hidden from her friends, and from herself. It was the only way – otherwise, they would destroy her.

London had been harder to live in than she'd imagined. Dark, at 3.30 pm, crowded subways full of people rushing and shoving to get where they needed to be, Cara would stand back and wait, but Sharon quickly worked out subway etiquette and tugged Cara along with her. Police and ambulance sirens filled the air day and night, and the bombing of a civilian plane over Lockerbie in Scotland four days before Christmas was too hard to comprehend.

The white Christmas didn't come. December 1988 was mild, with temperatures not falling below 7 degrees Celsius, and the plane disaster in Scotland filled the news, dampening Christmas festivities.

7 degrees was cold for Cara and her friends, and they enjoyed what they called a traditional British Christmas Dinner – roast

turkey and cranberry sauce with lots of roast veggies. A plum pudding with brandy sauce and silver coins for making wishes. They set it alight, pulled crackers and wore paper hats.

Cara watched the throngs at the Boxing Day sales on television, glad she'd stayed home, but Sharon returned full of excitement carrying bags with brand names she couldn't buy in Perth.

'Are you going to have a shower?' Sharon asked from the doorway.

The tour group was billeted in dormitory-style accommodation, possibly to save money; the room the girls shared had no ensuite.

'I want to finish this,' Elizabeth said from the bed where she sat writing.

'Is the bathroom empty?' Cara asked.

'Yes.'

'Is the water hot? Has it got a proper shower?' Liz asked absently.

Showers were something they had taken for granted; the flat they shared in Muswell Hill had a bathroom with a bath but only a handheld shower on a hose.

'Yes.'

'I'm going,' Liz said. She grabbed her toiletries and rushed out of the room.

'Down the hall, second on the right,' Sharon called after her. She rubbed her hair with a towel as she flopped on one of the three beds in the room. They were covered in identical doonas that matched the pink and green floral curtains in the windows. 'Do you think they're staying here?' she asked.

'What?' Cara turned from the window.

'The boys downstairs … do you think they're staying here?'

'I don't know.'

'They are cute.'

'Yes.'

'Maybe they'll be at dinner.' Sharon dragged a brush through her hair.

Cara looked at her friend. *You always do this. Why is it bothering me so much this time?*

Perhaps it was the letter.

Tommy Jenkins – they'd known each other for three years, and he'd said he loved her – had written to her – at least he did that – and told her he'd met a girl from Queensland and was moving interstate to be with her. He said he was sorry; she wouldn't have left him if she loved him. Did she expect him to wait for her?

After three years, maybe he was right. If she loved him, she wouldn't have gone … but he knew she was planning this trip; he could have waited; it was only for six months. Her heart broke when his letter arrived, but Tommy didn't know everything. Cara hadn't trusted him enough to tell him, so she couldn't have loved him.

Could she ever love anyone? Could anyone ever love her?

The door opened, and Liz said, 'Go and have a shower. It's wonderful.'

Cara pulled her backpack from under her bed and took out the essentials. She heard her friend ask, 'What's up?' as she headed down the warm hallway, but the bedroom door shut and she didn't hear Sharon's reply.

In the wood-lined dining room, Cara and her friends shared a long table covered with a floral cloth and set with chunky bowls and plates with the Contiki Tour group they were part of. Strangers occupied two tables in the room, and one table under a window was empty. The two men were not in the dining room, and Cara scolded herself; she was being silly. She had saved hard for this trip and was going to enjoy it, with her friends.

Chapter Two

Cara

Sunlight beamed through a porcelain blue sky, reflecting off the snow on the ground. Cara and her friends, dressed in hired ski outfits and boots, and holding hired skis, they looked the part as they gathered with the tour group for their first lesson.

Skiers moved gracefully around them; young children swished by, but the group Cara was part of, looked awkward and afraid.

'Hans, my name is Hans,' their instructor told them in heavily German-accented English. 'We will begin on the *baby slope*. Come now.'

Carrying unfamiliar equipment and slipping on alien terrain, they clomped behind Hans to a gentle slope on the snow-covered hillside. There, they learnt how to adjust their boots and put their skis on.

'Soon, you will be skiing down the slopes,' Hans said. He waved his hand in the direction of a gentle slope. There was nervous laughter from the group and more giggling as members of the group slipped, slid and tripped to the ground. They sat with legs extended and skis pointing skyward, arms not long enough to latch boots and skis together.

By lunchtime, Cara and her friends could stand on their skis, move forward and, most importantly, stop. The afternoon lesson was spent furthering these skills and learning to use a tow rope. The day ended with exhausted and bruised girls sitting by the fire before retiring early.

Two days later, under a sun that surprised Cara with its warmth, the girls were using tow ropes and skiing down reasonable slopes as Hans had predicted.

The group stood at the bottom of what they called the *big T bar*, and Hans said, 'We are going to the top, and we will ski down.'

'It's a long way up,' a valiant voice cried.

'Look at the *kinder*,' Hans said. 'They are only small, and they have been up there; come now.'

And they did.

The lift attendant instructed: 'Sit your body on the bar, feet in skis, lean backwards, holding your ski poles in one hand and the central bar in the other.'

Cara sat beside Sharon, her hand aching from gripping the central pole, unsure if she was terrified or excited as the lift pulled them up the snow-covered slope.

Cautiously skiing off the lift and onto the unloading area, avoiding Sharon and the others in the group, Cara exclaimed, 'I did it,' as she came to a halt.

Her hair blew out from under her beanie as she pushed her poles into the snow and hurtled down the mountain, unaware of the speed she was travelling until it was time to slow. *Snow plough,* she reminded herself. *That's what you've been taught. Front of your skis together in a V shape.*

It didn't work. She wasn't slowing down. But then the slope began to flatten, and she regained control, forced her skis into *snow plough* and began to slow.

She saw them—a group of five or six in her path.

Don't shout, don't embarrass yourself.

Cara jerked her skis left, but she clipped the back of a ski. One of the women in the group stumbled and slid ungainly to her backside, flurries of snow cascading around her.

Cara dropped her poles as she pitched forward, and threw her hands out to break her fall; she hit the snow, slid forward, and stopped in a crumpled heap. Her skis slid in behind her, and her poles glided in after them.

She heard a female voice snap, 'Stupid woman.'

'Are you hurt?' a male voice asked.

'No,' the woman said. 'But I've got snow all over me.'

'Snow?'

'Yes,' the woman growled.

Cara lifted her head to see the woman she'd tripped helped up. She saw the back of a navy ski jacket as he supported the woman, saw the woman flick snow from her trousers, and the anger on her face. Someone was talking to her.

'Are you alright?'

Cara turned into a sitting position, tugged her beanie straight and pushed her goggles onto her head. Putting her hand on the ground to help herself stand, she realised how slippery snow was.

She took the black-gloved hands that reached out to her, steadied herself, and heaved herself from the ground. She stood looking into the sapphire eyes she'd seen two days ago. 'Yes, I'm good. I'm sorry about this.' Her knees buckled under her. 'Maybe not.'

He held her arm, steadying her further. He was almost a stranger, yet he felt like she knew him or would like to know him. 'Is your friend alright? I'm so sorry,' Cara muttered.

He glanced towards the woman. She'd stomped away, leaving her skis behind; her companions, carrying their skis, trailed behind her. 'I think she's okay,' he said.

Cara stepped away from him as Liz and Sharon skied to a stop before her.

'Cara, are you alright?' Liz asked.

'Yes, just a little wobbly.'

'You should be more careful,' Liz scolded.

'Any damage?' Cara toppled headlong into golden-brown eyes. He wore a navy ski jacket. 'I'm fine. Did I hurt your friend? I'm sorry. I should say sorry,' she stuttered.

'Maybe later, she's not hurt and will be ….' A shadow fell over his face.

'Are you sure she's not hurt?'

'Yes, just a bit of snow …,' he said, placing his hand over his heart where she'd struck him with that snowball.

Cara plummeted into wild lilies. The world disappeared – they were alone on the mountain. He reached out, pushed a loose curl from her eyes, and brushed snow from her cheeks with the back of his fingers.

Cara traced her fingers on her cheek, unable to tear her eyes away from his. *What's happening?* She shuddered, forced herself away from him, and shook herself internally.

The tour group had gathered at the bottom of the slope, and there was lots of noise and chatter as people exchanged tales of skiing down the hill.

Cara turned her attention to the blue-eyed man as he asked, 'Can you make it back to the hostel?'

'I'm fine. I've got my friends, you look after your friends, thanks.'

'Okay then. Catch you later,' he said.

'I hope not,' Cara said and giggled, and he returned her laughter easily.

He joined the other man as he retrieved the woman's skis, strapped them to his, and tossed them over his shoulder. Then, they made their way across the snow-covered ground to the hotel.

'Well?' Sharon flippantly brushed Cara's cheek. 'Who are they?'

'I don't know,' Cara murmured.

'You're hopeless, Caz.'

Cara lifted her hand to her face; she could feel fingers on her cheek. 'Yes.'

'Come on,' Liz said. 'Let's get you back to the hotel.'

***

In a room decorated with wooden panels and what she thought was Bavarian-styled wallpaper, Cara sat on one of four leather chairs scattered around the room. Empty flower boxes were visible through the glass windows as the light from inside fell onto the snow-covered ground. She had pulled the burgundy chair close to the roaring fire and was writing letters and nursing bruises. A shadow fell across her page, and she looked up into blue eyes.

'Any injuries?' he asked.

'No, just some bruises. I think I should stick to swimming and bodyboarding.'

'I'm Jeremy Stonehouse,' he said and held out his hand.

Cara took it; it was warm, comfortable, and somehow familiar as he placed his other hand over hers.

'I'm Cara-Rose Maloney, most people call me Cara.'

'Nice to meet you, Cara Maloney.' A grin ran across his face, screwing up his eyes. He pulled a brown chair close to the fire and sat opposite her.

'Where do you swim and bodyboard?' he asked.

'Cottesloe beach.'

'In Western Australia?'

'Have you heard of it?'

'Yep, heard there is good surf there.'

'Not too bad. Where are you from?'

'San Francisco … you know where that is?'

'Yes, everyone's heard the song.'

He laughed and said, 'Not all of us wear flowers in our hair.'

He ran his hands through light brown curls.

Cara giggled at the image of him with flowers in his hair.

'Are the girls ….' a voice called from the hallway.

The brown-eyed man entered the room. Cara's fingers jumped to her cheek where he'd brushed the snow away earlier that day.

Jeremy stood, and Cara noticed their physical resemblance. They were the same height, six feet and a few inches. The shirts they wore tucked into their trousers emphasised lean, masculine bodies. They had similar faces, straight noses, and squarish chins. Jeremy had tanned skin, while the other man's skin was paler.

They were artistic copies of each other, copies the painter had altered, changing the eye colour and giving one lighter hair.

Jeremy wore a bomber jacket, open at the front. His hair sat untidily across his forehead, touching dark eyebrows. The other man had a sweater over his shoulders, his brown curls neatly gelled away from his face.

Cara asked, 'Are you brothers?'

'No,' Jeremy said. 'We get that sometimes; we're just friends.' He gestured to his friend. 'David, this is Cara-Rose Maloney, Cara, this is David Hayle.'

David shook her hand. She hoped he couldn't hear her heart beating.

'Hello, David,' she said.

'I am pleased to meet you, Cara-Rose Maloney,' David said. 'How are you now?'

'Just a little bruised,' she said. 'How is your friend?'

'She's okay.'

'That's good.'

'Cara's from Cottesloe,' Jeremy bounced around.

'Near Fremantle?' David asked.

Cara nodded. 'Have you been there?'

'Yes, we visited for The America's Cup.'

After Australia won the America's Cup Yacht Race in September 1983, the next challenge occurred in Fremantle in the summer of 86/87. It was a clean sweep for the American team, winning four races straight and taking the trophy back to America.

'Rich American tourist,' Cara teased.

'Just tourists,' he said. 'My mother ...,'

'David ... Jeremy,' a female voice called from the hallway. 'Are you coming?'

'Duty calls,' Jeremy said to Cara. 'Catch you later!'

'Coming,' he answered the voice in the hallway as he left the room.

David

David lingered. He sat on the brown chair beside her and asked, 'Are you staying here long?'

'Two weeks.' She ran her hand through her curls, they flickered like the coals burning in the fireplace. He wondered if he could run his hands through her curls – but mentally shook himself. What was he thinking– he should not do that.

She looked into his eyes. He'd never seen eyes like hers, emerald-green with blue flecks that sparkled in the firelight. They might hide a fiery temperament, but he saw gentleness, innocence, uncertainty, eyes hiding something he could not reach.

He didn't understand his actions earlier that day, why he'd pushed hair away from those eyes and brushed the snow from her face. Why did the world disappear when he did that?

'Two weeks,' she repeated. 'A skiing holiday, just a skiing holiday.'

She seemed confused and flustered. He was beginning to feel the same. He'd never felt unsure of himself, even as a teenager, he'd always been confident, known what to do.

Her eyes made the world reel around him; his heart thumped like he'd run a 100-metre sprint. Did her heart beat feel the same? Was he allowed to think that?

'David,' a female voice called.

He could hear Jeremy and the girls chattering in the hallway, – he had to leave. But he wanted to stay and sit by the fire with her and understand why she made him feel like his world was spinning away.

'David!' He was being summoned.

'I have to go,' he said, pushing himself off the chair. 'Maybe I'll see you later.'

Cara smiled. 'Maybe.'

Cara

When David joined his companions, Cara caught a glimpse of blonde hair and the back of a fur coat; it was real; it would have to be. She would not wear real fur even if she could afford it, such a horrible thing, to kill animals to make fashionable coats. The other two women in the group dressed the same.

She looked down at herself, old boots, jeans, and a jumper, not her best clothes, but even that would struggle to compare with what these women wore.

She heard chit-chat in the hallway before Sharon came twirling into the room, 'Well, who are they? Where are they from?'

Cara glanced at the doorway. 'David and Jeremy. They're from San Francisco.'

'Are you going to see them again?'

'I don't know … maybe.'

Sharon sighed. 'Are you coming out?'

'Not tonight.'

Sharon skipped away and joined the tour group gathering in the hallway. She seemed to have boundless energy and liked to party, but Cara was too tired after all that had happened.

Her fingers wandered to her face. David's touch when he shook her hand sent fire racing around her body, like earlier that day when he'd touched her cheek, making the world disappear and sending a flame up her spine. She'd never felt that before.

Perhaps Tommy meant this when he wrote:

> *'We were happy, Cara, because we didn't know any better. I hope we can still be friends, and I wish for you what I have found. When it happens, you will understand.*

Chapter Three

Cara

The blue skies of the previous day were now grey, and it was difficult to tell where land and sky separated. Cara sat on thick snow, struggling with her skis. She'd sent her friends on with the class, sure she could get back onto her feet quickly, and now she watched them disappear into the falling snow.

The swish of a skier coming to a halt where she sat startled her, and she looked into David Hayle's brown eyes as he pushed his goggles up onto his head. She could disappear in those eyes if she weren't careful.

'Having more trouble?' he asked.

'Just a little.'

'Let me help?' He clipped her skis onto her boots and held her hand as she stood and steadied herself. Even though they both wore gloves, quivers raced down her spine.

'I have to catch up with the class,' Cara stuttered.

'Want some company?'

Cara pulled her ski goggles over her eyes, tugged her beanie tight onto her head, and said, 'That would be nice.'

***

'There you are.' Elizabeth waved a greeting as Cara and David skied up to the front steps of the on-mountain restaurant, where the class had stopped for lunch. 'Hans was just about to send out a search party.'

Cara and David removed their skis and placed them and their poles in the rack provided. She flicked snow from her jacket and pulled off her gloves as she followed Liz back into the restaurant. Sharon looked up in surprise as David came through the door behind her. A space near the window at the end of the tour group's table was empty. David and Cara sat there. Cara turned her chair to face the fire and rubbed her hands together.

What was she doing? She'd never been so impulsive. She'd met Tommy just after she turned twenty-one when they shared a house with friends. Even then, she'd known him for twelve months before they moved into a place of their own.

Cara had only met David; she knew next to nothing about him except – he was attractive and handsome, like Gregory Peck in the old-time Hollywood movies she'd watched as a girl. Brown curls, those amazing dark eyes, a gentle heart-stirring smile, his accent adding to this.

She wasn't one of those sappy girls in the movies, all longing looks and fluttering eyelashes. But when David was near, her body tingled, unexpected thoughts ran through her head, and her heart jumped around in her chest.

It frightened her.

David

David pulled his chair close to Cara as she stared into the flames. When she'd tossed that snowball in his direction and gazed into his eyes, his world had scattered around him. He'd never experienced anything like that before, never felt so flustered. Cara had scurried away, leaving him bewildered.

When she slipped on the front step of the Pension and Jeremy helped her up, he'd felt a pang of envy. That wasn't right.

Jeremy had laughed with her as he stood lounging at the reception desk, and he'd heard Cara's giggle in return. But when he'd looked over his shoulder, she was staring at him, and he'd felt lost. He'd shaken himself, forcing her out of his mind, and concentrated on what he was doing.

That's what he thought he'd done.

What he should do?

But he kept meeting her.

Was it a casual attraction, a girl he'd met on holiday? With the turmoil in his life, he shouldn't get involved with anyone else, especially someone who confused him so much.

Cara looked into his eyes, and he was drowning in emerald pools. He would struggle to swim free if he wasn't careful.

He should stay away.

Cara

Cara could sense David distancing himself from her, maybe that was the right thing to do, the smart thing to do. He was a man she'd met on holiday, creating feelings she'd never had before. Was it just a physical attraction?

Could it be just physical?

Cara had never had a casual physical experience. Sex education at her Catholic Girls' School consisted of *don't*.

'We seem to be running into each other, don't we?' David said. His gaze wandered around the room, away from hers.

'Yes, it seems like it.'

His eyes settled on her. 'I don't know if I believe in fate, do you?'

No, no, I don't believe in fate.

'I don't believe in fate.' That was a step too far for Cara.

'I like to think we have control over our destiny.' David reasoned.

'I would agree with that.'

Can I control this?

A waiter interrupted them. Cara shrugged her shoulders and shook her head, unable to understand what she was asked. She turned to David as he said, 'He wants to know if you want anything to eat; you've missed the group's lunch order. Are you hungry … shall I order for you?'

Cara nodded, and David ordered food.

'The class is leaving,' Sharon called from the middle of the table. 'We're heading back to the hotel.' She sauntered down to the end of the table where Cara and David sat, her brows raised, quizzing Cara. Cara introduced her friend to David, glad of the distraction.

'I can see Cara back if that's okay with her.' David glanced at Cara.

'That's fine.' Cara smiled. Food was brought to the emptying table. 'Can't let food go to waste.'

Liz stood beside the table, looked into Cara's eyes, and said without words *take care*, 'Yes, Mama…' Cara nodded and smiled. 'All good. I'll see you at the hotel.'

The restaurant emptied as Cara and David shared their food, chatting and keeping the conversation in safe territory. Cara finished the broth David had called Tafelspitz. It tasted of beef and root vegetables and was served with apples mixed with a sharp tangy flavour she did not recognise. She drank her coffee and finished every bite of her sweet cinnamon spiced apple strudel, thankful for all the exercise skiing gave her.

'Would you like to go skiing before we return to the hotel?' David asked.

'What about your friends? Won't they wonder where you are?'

'Jeremy's a big boy; he can look after himself, and the girls have gone to Vienna to shop. So, I'm all by myself.' He touched his heart and smiled at her and, like the silly song said, her heart went *boom de boom*.

Cara looked out the window, where snow was no longer falling, but the grey sky seemed heavy, and the wind bent naked tree branches to the ground. 'Is the weather alright?' she asked.

'I'll find out.'

Destiny.

She did not believe in that. She didn't want to get involved with another man, not yet, not after Tommy; she didn't want that heartache again.

David returned from the reception desk at the front of the restaurant. 'The mountain is still open. We should get at least one more run if you like.'

'Sounds good.'

***

Halfway up the mountain, snow began to fall, and the wind buffeted the chairlift high above the white ground, shaking it violently. Cara reached for David's gloved hand and clutched it tightly; he pulled her close, and she leaned into his body for security. It didn't help. The chair rattled around like it was falling to pieces.

When the lift reached the top of the mountain, Cara stumbled as she skied onto the unloading area. They were not the last riders on the chairlift, and David helped her move out of the way of oncoming skiers. He sat her on a seat before he spoke to the lift attendant. Cara could see other skiers staying on the lift or returning to the chairlift instead of skiing down the mountain.

Snow swirled around David's legs as he walked back to her. 'The storm's getting worse; the mountain is closing. We should get back while we can. We can take the lift back or ski down before it gets too bad. Or we could wait for the storm to pass, but it might not.'

'Not the lift.' Cara shuddered. She didn't want to get back on that wonky thing. She saw other skiers making their way down the slopes, and there were glimmers of sunshine reflecting on the white snow. 'Let's ski back.'

The wind died down as they began their descent. Cara had been right: sunshine splattered the slopes; the restaurant was in sight, and soon they would be on their way to the ski slopes near the hotel. Suddenly the restaurant disappeared, sleet swirled around them, and the world became white.

Cara lost control of her skis and tripped, her hand reaching out to emptiness. She fought to stay upright, but falling snow and wind drove her down into the white powder. Her hand searched for solid ground, but she fell even deeper into the snow. Howling wind tore at her hair and threw ice into her face.

She managed to push herself upright, but couldn't stay on her feet and collapsed, tumbling into the snow. She felt very cold, and suddenly she also felt tired. How long had she been in this storm? – it felt like forever. Exhausted, she stopped fighting the storm, considering she would rest a while and then get up and try and find her way home.

Cara felt herself pulled to her feet and shaken. 'I'm tired,' she mumbled. 'Let me sleep, then I'll get up.' She shoved the hands, helping her away.

'No, Cara, come on; it's not time for sleep,' David said. 'We have to keep going.'

'No …'

'Yes! Cara, we have to keep going. The restaurant can't be far … it's not far, just downhill.' David's words were barely audible above the storm. He held her close and forced her to move.

She stumbled, protesting, but he ignored them. The shrieking wind cut through her clothing – *snow should be soft* – but this snow seemed to slice into her skin.

Then David slipped and fell, pulling Cara down with him. Over the screeching wind, she heard him mumble, 'Tired, tired.'

Cara lifted her head; she could see lights flickering through the falling snow, and realised the savage wind seemed calmer. She urged David, tugging at him, but he didn't respond. Cara felt even more tired, and closed her eyes. *Sleep, everything will be alright after sleep.*

***

Jeremy Stonehouse paced the foyer of the Pension Frieden, and those who shared the floor with him moved aside. He wrenched the front door open and stomped out into the sleeting snow, and stared up at the mountain–the invisible mountain, its slopes covered by a raging storm, a complete whiteout.

The sky, the chair lift, the mountain peak were all covered by a fierce blizzard. 'Damn you, David Hayle; you better be out of this storm.'

Upstairs, Cara's two friends clutched each other's hands as they stared out a window at the storm-covered mountain.

Chapter Four

Cara

Cara sat before a roaring fire, curled in David's arms, sharing his body heat. She felt like she would never be warm again.

David held a glass of warm wine to her lips. 'Drink this. We're safe now.'

She drank the wine too fast, spluttering at the taste. David gulped his down and pulled a blanket tight around them.

Outside, the wind screamed, tree branches groaned and pounded on the wooden window shutters as the raging storm threw snow and ice against them. Behind closed shutters, the storm noise dulled. Firelight filled the room, wood cracked and burned, and sparks fell on the stone hearth and faded out.

Cara shuddered; she'd fallen asleep in the blizzard, but David had struggled to his feet, dragged her off the ground, and forced her to her feet. She'd pushed him away, but he'd held her upright and pulled her close, making her move.

A lull in the storm had given them time to reach the restaurant. They'd pounded on the closed door and found refuge inside, the owner giving them blankets and warm wine and offering his spare room for the night.

Her lips were chaffed, and she could feel a cold spot on her cheek, and nothing was warming her. Another glass of warm wine made her drowsy, and she snuggled deep into David's arms. She would share a room with David tonight.

But something was happening that she didn't understand; she'd always been sensible, always had a steady head. Sharon was the flighty, romantic one, not her. She'd had too much wine – could she make a sensible decision?

She pushed herself out of David's arms, but he ran a finger down her cheek. 'You're safe now.'

He was delightfully warm and, feeling the cold surround her again, she snuggled back into his arms.

***

Cara woke clothed in her camisole and knickers, the warm male body, his arm slung over her hip was clothed. She shifted onto her elbow, and he rolled on his back, the doona slipping. He wore a white t-shirt and black boxer shorts – he'd shared her bed, not her body. She sighed, relieved. She'd drunk too much wine but not enough to make an unsafe decision.

David's mussed-up hair fell over his forehead and his chest rose and lowered gently. She wondered what it would be like to have her mouth on his, hold his naked body against hers. She'd never made the first move before: Tommy had always taken the lead.

Turning onto her back, Cara's red hair tangled around her face. She pushed the curls away, and David stirred.

He rolled to face her. 'Good morning. Are you feeling better?'

'Mmm.' She ran the back of her fingers against his stubbly cheek and he pulled her close and took her face in his hands. Her dry lips softened as he ran his tongue around them. When he gently sought her tongue, she opened her lips. Cara ran her tongue across his, her hands seeking his body, wanting his body. She'd never been so bold.

She pulled his t-shirt over his head, ran her fingers through the brown hair on his toned chest, and pushed his shorts down.

He pushed the straps from her camisole down, caressing her breasts with his tongue, chewing her nipple. Cara sucked in air, holding him to her breasts. She ran her fingers through his hair and stroked the back of his neck.

'We shouldn't,' David muttered. 'I can't.' He wrenched himself from her throbbing body, breathing raggedly.

'Maybe not,' Cara whispered.

David heaved his legs over the side of the bed and pulled his shorts on. He sat with his shoulders rigid.

Cara pulled the sheets up under her chin and stared at his back. Reckless with desire, she knew she could run her hands across his shoulders, down his spine, and pull him back into the bed, make love with him, let him make love with her. She could do that.

He would come to her if she did.

But she did not.

Chapter Five

In a room upstairs in the Pension Frieden, Jeremy Stonehouse and David Hayle argued. Both knew they were right, and both knew they were wasting words.

At the same time, two friends argued in another room on the other side of the hotel.

Cara

'Where did you spend last night?' Sharon Peterson demanded. *Why does Sharon always have to know everything?*

'David called you.'

'Yes.'

'We got caught in the storm. The restaurant owner had a spare room.' Cara didn't want to talk about this, it was none of Sharon's business.

'With David?'

'Yes.' Cara closed her eyes.

'He's not your type, Cara.'

Sharon thinks she knows everything about men. 'What do you mean, *my type*?'

'He's obviously very well off, and you don't know anything about him.'

Cara was going to say, what did it matter, but it was all too hard, so she said, 'He wears nice clothes.'

'They are not nice, Cara; they are very expensive.'

Sometimes, Sharon can be so shitty. 'You would know.'

'Yes, I would.' Sharon placed a hand gently on Cara's shoulder. 'I don't want you to get hurt.'

I'm already hurt – Maybe Sharon's right, I barely know David, and should stay away from him … but…. 'Nothing happened, Sharon. We didn't … he didn't want to.'

Tears welled in Cara's eyes, spilled over the rims, and rolled down her cheeks. *Did I make a fool of myself this morning?*

Sharon pulled her into her arms, and held her gently. 'Aww, sweet girl, it's alright.'

Cara took comfort in her friend's arms before she pulled away and wiped her cheeks with the back of her hand like she was seven years old.

And then she was seven years old, clutching Sharon's hand at the wire gate, promising they would always be friends.

'Come now, Sharon, say goodbye,' the lady in the pink floral dress with yellow hair said.

'Promise,' Cara asked. And Sharon promised. She'd kept that promise, but not until they were in high school. Cara hadn't seen Sharon again for five years. She'd watched the back of her friend as she clutched her little brown suitcase and walked away with that lady.

The sun moved across a pale blue sky. Shadows from the red brick building fell across her and she stood at that gate until it got cold.

When Sister Dominica came to get her, Cara looked up at her and asked, 'Why doesn't my mummy come and get me?'

Sister Dominica didn't answer, but she held Cara's hand gently as they made their way up the brick steps under a sign that read, Perth Home for Girls.

Sharon squeezed Cara's fingers. 'That's not always a bad thing.'

'No?'

'No, sometimes it's better not to go too far.' Sharon sighed. 'Believe me, I know. Especially if it's real.'

'Maybe.'

'Don't fight,' a voice from the other bed said.

Both girls turned to their friend, Liz, who had tears running down her face as she read a letter.

No! Cara's heart broke. Tommy Jenkins was right, she knew now they hadn't loved each other. But Elizabeth and Mike had been together since high school and had always planned their lives together. He'd promised to wait for her, but he had to finish his studies and wanted her to have her holiday. Was he abandoning her? Telling her he no longer loved her in a letter?

'Mike asked me to marry him.' Liz smiled as tears ran down her cheeks. 'He's going to defer his final year and come over so we can be together.'

Three friends shared hugs and kisses. Among all her confusion, Cara found happiness for her dear friend.

Chapter Six

David

David Hayle stood on skis at the top of the slope. He could see Cara sitting alone at one of several wooden tables on the side porch of the Pension Frieden, sheltered from the wind and warmed by the sunshine. A halo of golden curls fell around her shoulders.

He'd argued with Jeremy that morning, and knew Jeremy was right. He shouldn't get involved with Cara. His life was complicated at the moment, and he shouldn't involve anyone else in it.

He didn't believe in fate or destiny, but yesterday, when he found her struggling with her skis as her class disappeared … she seemed to crash into his life unexpectedly. When he thought his efforts to forget her, to put her out of his mind had succeeded, he would see her again. What was that?

He dusted his navy and white ski suit, pulled his goggles over his eyes, and pushed himself down the slope. He loved skiing. His grandparents often brought the family here when he was a child, and happy memories of those times filled him with joy.

As he skied to a halt where Cara sat, he realised the simple joy he'd felt when skiing with his grandfather; the first time he'd made it down this slope without falling … that's how Cara made him feel. But he'd been six years old that day – he'd be twenty-seven on his next birthday – a man with responsibilities and obligations.

Cara looked up from the book she was reading, and squinted in the sunlight reflecting off the white ground. The sprinkling of freckles across her nose and cheeks stood out in the sunshine.

David remembered her body in his arms that morning, so pale where the sun had never touched; how he'd wanted her. But he wouldn't sleep with Cara; it couldn't be just sex with her. He knew that. Casual sex often left him feeling empty. It would be more with Cara.

His parents' love for each other had filled his life. The love his grandparents shared. What would it feel to love like that? He'd been in love, or what he called love – it was nothing like what they had.

He pushed his ski goggles onto his head. 'Hi.'

'Hi.' Cara closed her book and shaded her eyes from the glare with her hand. He was sinking into that glittering pool. She would see his soul if he let her.

'May I join you?' he asked.

'Yes.' Cara nodded.

He unclipped his skis, stood them and the poles next to the table, and sat opposite her. 'Not skiing this afternoon?'

'No, still a bit cold from yesterday.' She rubbed her hands together, and he saw a shadow cross her face as she remembered the storm. They had been lucky.

He tugged his gloves off, reached over, took her cold hands and held them gently. 'We're safe.'

'Mmm.' Cara's hands trembled as he held them. 'It was a bit silly.'

'It was, but we are okay. Are you hungry?'

Cara looked into his eyes, and he could see she was uncertain and didn't understand what had happened that morning. He was fighting to understand it himself. The battle threatened to overwhelm him, and he said, 'I'm sorry about this morning.'

She stared at their joined hands before pulling away and picking up the menu. 'Yes, I'm hungry,' she burst out as a waiter approached the table.

I'm making a hash of this; I want to talk to her, explain, if that's possible. Cara looked blankly at the menu, so he ordered food and warm wine for them both.

The patio started filling with skiers returning from the slopes for lunch. Luckily, they had ordered before the rush and shared food and light conversation when their meals arrived.

He'd always known the direction his life would take: finish high school, and graduate from college. Not good enough for the first team, but good enough for the starting five of the second College Basketball team. He would work for his father, advance into upper management, marry, and have three children, a girl and two boys, to carry on his father's name. He thought he was on his way to doing that.

As he sat opposite Cara, her curls moving in the breeze and her eyes looking into his, it struck him, that was his father's life. Cara had reached into his heart, she was like no one he'd ever met, and she caused him to question everything he thought he wanted.

Could he have a different life, his own life, or was it too late?

My own life.

David looked across the table. 'Will you come to dinner with me tonight?'

Cara hesitated. 'I would like that.'

***

The next day, David and Cara stood at the bottom of the chairlift, poles in hand, skis on feet. He watched her chew her bottom lip as the seat came around.

'It's not stormy,' he said and took her hand. As the chairlift scooped them off the ground, he pulled the safety bar down, and they rose into the sky. David saw Cara look around. He couldn't see her eyes behind her goggles, but he sensed her fear and pulled her close to his body.

Cara looked up at him before nestling in close. When the ride reached the unloading area, he felt Cara relax. She skied away from the chair onto the gentle slope.

***

David and Jeremy spent the next three days with Cara and her friends. She regained her confidence in the snow, and he learnt about her. She'd been educated at a Catholic girls' school but hadn't attended university. She worked in a store in Perth, and he told her he also worked in his father's store in San Francisco.

David told her he was travelling with his sisters. The younger one, Elyse, was celebrating her 21st birthday, and he was the big brother keeping them safe on a tour of Europe.

When he asked about her family, her eyes filled with tears. 'My parents died in a car crash when I was very young.' He held her close; said he was sorry. 'It was long ago,' she said. 'I never knew them.' She didn't want to talk about her family after that.

On Saturday night, he and Jeremy joined the tour group Cara and her friends were part of for a torchlight hike. David was astounded by the effect the fire in the torches and the quiet darkness of the forest had on the tour group. They were a rowdy bunch, drinking and singing most nights, but now they walked through the forest in hushed silence. An occasional whisper could be heard, and when the tour came out from under the forest canopy, there were quiet gasps as the stars appeared to be falling all around them.

He held Cara with her back to him, her body pressing against his; she was almost a foot shorter than him, and his arms wrapped around her easily. Cara caressed his arms as he held her, and when she turned her head and looked up at him, torchlight reflected in her eyes, burning his soul.

On Sunday, he went to Vienna and did the hardest thing he'd ever done.

Chapter Seven

Cara

On Wednesday, after spending the morning sightseeing and window-shopping, David and Cara sat in a café in St Johann.

David had spent two nights in Vienna. He'd returned quieter and appeared disturbed. Cara wanted to ask him what had happened, but he smiled across the table as a pianist played *The Blue Danube*. The melody drifted across the typical Tyrol room, with its wood panelled walls and ceiling and woollen rugs on the floor. Even though it was lunchtime, the dance floor was occupied by couples enjoying the music, and Cara watched Jeremy and Sharon twirl around the dance floor.

'Come on,' David siad, offering her his hand.

Cara took it, expecting him to take her to the dance floor, but he guided her to the coat check and grabbed their coats before hurrying her out of the café. Outside, he waved down a horse-drawn cab, helped her up, and pulled a fur blanket around her legs. Cara snuggled into him, glancing at his face.

'What?' she asked.

'Nothing.' He shook his head, pulled her closer and kissed her lips.

There *was* something.

The horse pranced along cobblestones, clopping hooves echoing off the stone buildings surrounding them. The cab stopped in front of what appeared to be a castle – an old stone building with turrets covered in snow, its windows surrounded by red shutters reflecting the weak sunshine.

'We can be on our own,' David told her. 'And the food is not too bad either.'

They climbed the stone stairs and opened a heavy wooden door into a fantasy land. Cara stared at the scene before her. Hundreds of lights adorned the ceiling of the huge room, and a timber staircase led up to the next floor. Velvet and leather furniture sat on plush red and green carpet.

David led her onto a wooden balcony, and Cara pulled her coat tight. He put his arm around her and gestured to a waiter before guiding her to a table where Cara could see naked tree branches reflecting off the surface of a lake. She turned as the air behind her warmed, grateful for the gas heater on the wall.

Steaming wine and a cheese fondue were placed on the table. A ceramic bowl full of bubbling cheese, chunks of fresh bread, and thin forks reminded her she hadn't eaten. A plate of meat sliced and diced and what looked like beef soup to Cara were also placed on the table. David moved his chair so he was sitting beside her, and they ate, watching the shadows grow longer.

Evening hovered around on the ride through a winter wonderland back to the Pension Frieden. David helped Cara down from the carriage, and she tumbled into his arms.

In the empty living room of the Pension, they pulled chairs in front of the roaring fire. Cara rubbed her hands together and looked at David, that quiet, disturbed look back on his face. What had happened?

'I have something I want you to know,' he said.

Cara's heart jumped, *something you want me to know.*

'Where the hell have you been?' Jeremy Stonehouse demanded from the doorway of the living room.

'Don't make a fuss,' David said.

Jeremy said no more, but he turned to the three women standing in the doorway behind him.

David stiffened as the women looked at them. David's sisters, one with long brown hair and clear tanned skin, another with light brown curls and the same eyes as David. But the one that startled Cara was the beautiful blonde girl she'd knocked over on the ski slope. She stared at David like she owned him, and glared at Cara with so much hatred that Cara gasped for air.

Cara had seen hate directed at her from other eyes before. She fled the room, pushing past those standing in the doorway, ran down the hallway, through the foyer, and out the front door. She ran across the torch-lit snow, hearing curses she did not understand as she caused skiers to swerve. She had to get away from the building, away from him.

Until a hand stopped her as David grasped her arm. 'Cara.'

Frozen air blew around her and torch lights flickered. A storm was coming down the mountain and she wanted to run into it and keep running. She'd been stupid, stupid. Why had she thought it was more than a holiday fling?

'Don't touch me.' She shrugged his hand away.

'I wanted you to know...' David released his grip, and Cara turned to face him. He stood before her, his eyes wet with tears.

'What, David? What do you want me to know?'

'I told Alice ...,' his words flew around her. 'We broke up.'

'What? When?'

'December. We broke up in December. I told her on Sunday I wasn't coming back.'

'Sunday?'

Sunday

The days they'd spent together, the memories they'd made and yet she knew. She'd tried to pretend she didn't see David holding himself back and fighting with himself, now she knew why.

At least he hadn't slept with her.

'I had to tell Alice – she wanted a *break*. But I knew she expected to get back together. I couldn't be with you until … I told her …. I couldn't … I had to do the right thing.'

'The right thing, David, would have been to leave me alone.' Cara snapped.

David wrapped his hands around hers. 'Would it? I wasn't looking for you, Cara. What could I do?'

'I don't know.' Icy tears burnt her cheeks; she flicked them away.

'Come inside, it's cold.' He held her hand gently.

Wind surrounded them, and snow began to fall; light faded as torches blew out. Cara stumbled, and he put his arms around her. She would have told him everything, all the things she'd never told anyone else. She breathed in his scent – cinnamon and nutmeg in his cologne; his body too close for her, she pulled out of his arms.

Snow fell thicker. The wind screeched. The only light outside now coming from the windows of the Pension. They needed to get out of the storm.

'Please, Cara. Come inside, you'll freeze out here.'

He put his hand on her back and guided her through the storm to the Pension. On the front step, he took her face in his hands, and all she could see were golden-brown eyes filled with tears. 'I didn't know I could feel like this – I'm sorry.'

'David, I …' Cara stared into his eyes, her legs trembling and her heart breaking.

'I'm sorry,' he repeated.

'So am I.' Cara forced herself away from him, turned and raced inside. She staggered upstairs, thankful the other girls had gone on the road trip to see the sights from the *Sound of Music* movie.

She couldn't cry, that might have helped, but no tears fell. There was just an empty nothing. She sat on the bed and watched the storm pour metres of snow on top of the already snow-covered ground.

Chapter Eight

Cara

Cara squinted as she walked out into bright sunlight from where she'd been feeding the horses in the barn under the Pension. The horses were big, gentle creatures, but living in a confined space meant she could only spend a short time with them before she needed air. She usually took sugar cubes from the breakfast table, but she hadn't eaten this morning, so the horses only had feed.

All the while, she tried to make sense of what had happened – it felt so much more than a holiday romance, but what would she know? She wanted to be angry, hurt, sad; she wanted to cry and scream. *Sharon's right: I know nothing about David and should have left it that way.*

'I want to talk to you.'

Cara blinked and looked at the woman approaching her - straight blonde hair, blue eyes, clear skin, high cheekbones, a nose that turned up at the end, dressed in a fur coat … *So perfect for David.*

Cara felt awkward and frumpy. 'Why?' she asked.

'What do you know about David?' The woman stepped closer.

What do I know about David? The time we have spent together, I think I can trust him. Have I been a fool? Cara stood her ground, 'I know he works in his family's store in San Francisco.'

'You are stupid,' the woman Cara knew to be Alice snapped. 'You know nothing about him! His father is a wealthy man. He doesn't own a store; he owns one of the biggest stores on the West Coast. When we marry, our families will own one of the largest retail empires in the country.'

'He told me you'd broken up ….'

Alice shoved her right hand in front of Cara's face. 'He gave this to me, a promise of the ring to come. No one will ever give you a ring like this. Do you think he would do that if we broke up?'

Cara spluttered, 'I don't … I … thought.'

'Do you think David Hayle would give up his whole future for a little tramp he met on holiday?' Alice spat the words at her.

Cara stifled her anger and took a deep breath. 'I'm not a ….'

'Do you think he could care about you?' Alice cut her off. 'Like in a fairy tale, the prince charming coming to rescue you from your dull life.'

The cold words cut Cara. She'd heard hateful words before, but this was different. These words, the rage in them, made her skin crawl, but Cara hadn't been afraid of words since she was a child. She turned to walk away.

Alice grabbed her arm. 'You have nothing in common with David. I have everything he could need and want. What can you give David?'

Nothing. I can give him nothing, not even the truth.

'Alice,' Jeremy called as he walked towards the two women.

Alice leant forward, her face close to Cara, her blue eyes cold steel. 'David is mine,' she hissed. 'He has always been mine and will always be mine. You will not take him away from me.'

Cara stepped back. She remembered the desolation Tommy's letter had filled her with, but it was nothing like this. She had cried and been angry, but she had not felt the level of hate Alice aimed at her.

Alice spun to face Jeremy. 'Explain it to her. You know all about love and loving the wrong person.'

Cara watched Alice's back as she stormed away, being careful not to slip on the icy ground. She turned to Jeremy. He screwed up the corner of his mouth as he stood staring after her.

***

Cara sat opposite Jeremy. They had walked in silence along the snow-covered ground to the small village near the Pension. He ordered warm strudel, which Cara pushed around her plate, and hot coffee, which she drank too fast, her chest aching with pain. The fire in the hearth flared, and sparks fell on the woollen rug to fizzle out.

'I thought David cared for me.'

Jeremy reached across the table and took her hand. 'He more than cares for you, Cara, but it's not going to be easy with Alice. I should have kept you and David apart.'

Cara looked into Jeremy's gentle blue eyes and remembered the first time she had done that. 'Do you think you could have?'

'It's too late now.' Jeremy squeezed her hand, and Cara nodded.

'Is it true about David's family?'

'Yes.'

Sharon was right.

'It doesn't change things.'

'Yes, it does.'

'Why?'

'For all the reasons Alice said.' Cara exhaled. Then she asked, 'Why are you here, Jeremy? If David is so rich, why are you at this little Pension in a backwater part of the Alps? Why aren't you in Saint Moritz or somewhere like that, with all the other wealthy people? Not here with us poor Contiki tourists.'

'David came here with his grandparents when he was a child. His grandfather commanded a submarine during the war, and one of his men's family members owns the pension. It's a family thing David wants to support. That's why the girls stay at a Spa Resort in St Johann and go to Vienna to shop and spend money.'

'What about you, Jeremy?' Cara took a breath. 'You're not a rich man's son, are you?'

'No.' He smiled. 'My father owns a small store near Milwaukee; he sells pipes and rakes and hoses.'

'How did you meet David?'

'I won a scholarship, *The Hayle Family Business Scholarship* to Berkley, an opportunity of a lifetime,' he quoted. 'I met David, and my life changed.'

'You aren't unhappy?' Cara questioned.

'No. I got a great education….' He hesitated like he was going to tell her something else. 'David and I became friends, like brothers; brothers who chose each other. But San Francisco is a long way from Milwaukee.'

'It's a lot further from Perth.'

'Yes.' The look on Jeremy's face told her David had walked into the café. He stood, kissed her cheek, and whispered, 'I know you love him.'

Cara noticed the two men exchange glances as they walked past each other, and then David slid into the seat opposite her.

He took his Ray-Bans off. The small lines under his golden-brown eyes showed he hadn't slept much last night. Clean-shaven, he'd gelled his hair back. He wore brown trousers and a woollen jumper over a crisp cream shirt, matched with a tan knee-length woollen coat. She should have noticed, should have paid attention to what Sharon said.

Cara pulled her secondhand, brown suede coat with the fake sheepskin collar together. She wore her brand-new marigold cashmere sweater, bought especially for the trip, for the *après ski*, and clutched her hands together over her denim jeans, sure her sleepless night showed on her face too.

'Can I talk to you?' David raked his fingers through his hair, and strands fell across his forehead. He brushed them away before staring into her eyes.

Cara pushed the tiredness from under her eyes, turned her gaze to her hand, fidgeted on the table before looking back at him. 'Yes, you can talk to me.'

'I saw you with Alice this morning.' His voice broke, and he reached across the table. 'I hope she didn't offend you. She can be difficult.'

Cara snatched her hands away and choked back a laugh. 'Is that what you call it? Probably not a good choice of words.' His gaze flitted around the room.

Cara sighed and ran her hand around her shoulder, shaking her head.

'I'm sorry.' He swallowed. 'I wanted to tell you.' Anguish ripped at his words. 'I didn't want this to happen.' David's eyes were misty, and it took all Cara's willpower not to reach out and run her fingers across his cheek.

'Will you let me tell you now?'

She nodded.

He took a deep breath. 'Alice is my sister's friend. Our parents are business associates. She has always been in my life. We went out in high school, went to the Prom, and saw each other as part of a group during our college years. We've been a couple on and off since college ....' He shook his head like he was trying to make sense of what he was saying. 'We got back together and planned to get engaged – it seemed what we should do – and everyone was happy. I thought I was happy; I thought I was in love.'

He dropped his head before pulling himself upright and saying, 'When Alice was offered work in Milan early in December, I told her we could wait, but she wanted to *take a break*, whatever that's supposed to mean. She expected me to wait for her, she always does.'

He breathed, steadying his voice, and pushed his trembling fingers under his eyes. 'The girls planned this trip for Elyse's birthday months ago.' He looked into Cara's eyes. 'Then ... then I met you.'

Cara wanted to soothe those hands, take them in hers, caress them. Instead, she tucked her hands safely under her knees.

'I told Alice I didn't want to get back together. She seemed to understand ... was I stupid to think she did?'

'Yes, you were.'

'I just wanted it to be simple.'

'Life's not like that, David.' Cara knew life wasn't simple. But as she looked at David, she thought maybe it was for him and wondered what that would be like: a simple, easy life.

'I want to know you, Cara. I want to be with you.' He swept his fingers along his cheeks.

A little tramp he met on holiday. Alice's words.

'We don't know anything about each other, maybe it's better ...' Cara looked away unable to get the words out.

David moved his chair around beside her. 'I thought I loved Alice; what we had was love, but it wasn't. It's just what ... what I thought was love.'

He was too close. She was defenceless.

He bowed his head before looking deep into her eyes. 'I tried to stay away from you. I didn't want to hurt Alice ... I had to tell her ... before ....'

There was no need for words here; he was telling her he would not sleep with her; it wouldn't be just sex with her.

Cara caught her breath. It could never be just sex for her, either.

'You made me realise I could have a different life. My own life, not a life I think my family wants, or a life to fulfil obligations. I could be happy and live the life I wanted.'

He reached across the table, but Cara kept her hands where they were, away from his touch. She wanted to stay in control, and she would lose that if she touched him.

'What about all the plans for you and Alice?' she asked.

'I thought that was what I wanted. I hope Alice will be happy. That she'll find someone to love, to love her in return.' He shook his head and said, 'I can't do that now.'

Cara shuddered, remembering the hate in Alice's eyes. His life was so different from hers. *Too different?*

'What will your family say? Can you walk away from *one of the biggest retail empires?*'

'If I have to.'

'You've never been short of money, David; you're a rich man's son; how will you live?'

'I can work.'

'Doing what?'

'I work in my father's store.' A wry smile crossed his lips.

'But … your family?'

'It will be okay, Cara. I am a grown man. I don't need my parents' permission for my life choices. I didn't know I could feel like this about anyone.' He sucked in air and rubbed his hand across his chest. 'It … sucks ….'

'I know.'

'Can you forgive me for falling in love with you?' He broke off, eyes wide, a guarded smile on his lips. 'I thought you loved me … am I wrong?'

Cara shook her head, 'You aren't wrong, but ….'

'Don't say but.' He reached for her hands, and this time, Cara gave them to him. She let him into her heart and her soul.

It was not safe to do that, but she did it anyway.

Chapter Nine

Cara

'Are you sure?' Cara asked.

'I should be asking you that.' David smiled gently, the uncertainty of the day hanging in the air. They stood in his room, curtains drawn as daylight began to wane. It was 4:00 p.m. The early nights were something Cara would never get used to. 'I'm sure.'

David pulled her into his arms and lowered his head to hers. 'So am I.'

Cara felt him relax and let go. He lifted her marigold jumper and camisole over her head and unclipped her bra. The straps fell from her shoulders, and the bra dropped to the floor.

She helped David unbutton his cream shirt, and it joined her bra on the floor. Her fingers traced along his chest, down his belly to his trousers. He sucked in a breath as her fingers wandered around the top button of his pants. He let them fall to the ground, stepped out of them, bundled her up and carried her to the bed. Lying beside her, he ran his fingers over her breasts and down her stomach. His fingers fumbled with her jeans before he pushed them down and tossed them on the floor.

***

Cara lay entwined in David's arms, astonished; she never knew lovemaking could be like this. She didn't think she could trust anyone with her body as she had done with David.

He'd left the lamp on low. She'd been uncertain about that, her heart racing, but when he lifted his head, she saw in his eyes tenderness and safety and knew she could trust him. She'd been engrossed watching him make his way around her body and helped him with the condom, and then he came to her. David found his way into her body and her soul.

Later, as their breathing slowed and their bodies calmed, Cara rested her head on his chest and listened to his heartbeat as she drifted away.

David

David opened his eyes. Cara slept with her head on his chest, breathing softly. Her red curls tickled his nose, and he pushed them gently away from his face.

She'd been shy about leaving the lamp on: she'd only ever had one lover she'd told him, and they never left the light on. He'd twisted his fingers through her red curls and traced the side of her face, the curve of her cheek, and her slightly rounded chin. His fingers caressed her breasts, ran across her smooth belly and between her legs, and then his mouth followed that line.

His father had taught him, *If she says no, that is what she means.* He would never ask for anything she wasn't comfortable with; he would not ask for anything she didn't want to give. He'd lifted his head and looked into her eyes. She smiled gently and nodded once before caressing the back of his neck and guiding him.

Her fingers were unsure as she helped him, and then they were together, Cara pulling him tightly into her, holding him like she would never let him go, and he never wanted to let her go.

He thought he'd made love before; but he was wrong; he never knew he could give so much of himself to anyone. So much more than physical contact, he understood now. How foolish he'd been to think he'd been in love. He would never have known if he hadn't met Cara.

He stroked her curls, breathed in her perfume, her essence. She stirred, moving into the crook of his arm. Slowly, she blinked her eyes open and gazed into his. And he knew he was right, no matter the consequences, no matter what happened, they would be together.

Cara turned onto her back, and he raised himself onto his elbow to look down on her.

'That was nice,' she said.

'Nice.' He gently slapped his chest and dropped his head, feigning hurt.

'There are so many words, David, awesome, amazing, brilliant, wonderful, Supercalifragi …'

He cut her words off, kissing her mouth, and felt the smile on his lips as she reached around his neck, returning his kisses.

When he could speak, he said, 'Nice is good.'

The flecks of blue in her eyes caught the lamplight. How glad he was she let him leave the light on so he could see her, and she could see him.

He'd been in and out of the relationship with Alice, and there had been other women in his life, but Cara would be the last woman he loved.

'I love you, Cara.' Those words came so easily, so naturally. She didn't understand how she had changed his life, and that was alright; they would find out about each other together. 'No matter what,' he said. 'I love you.'

Cara looked into his face. 'Since the first time I looked into your eyes, David, I loved you.' He rolled onto his back, and she curled into his chest, and he folded her tightly in his arms.

***

David woke with Cara asleep in his arms. He moved her gently, swung his legs over the side of the bed, pulled on his shorts and t-shirt, and made a phone call.

He sat on the bed and watched her sleep. She'd rolled onto her belly, and the ugly scar on her right shoulder sneered at him, making his heart race. It was an old scar but must have been a serious injury.

How had it happened?

He traced his fingers in the air over it.

The knock on the door woke Cara. She turned onto her back, pushed her red hair away from her face, sat, and pulled the blanket up over her breasts. Glancing around the room, her surprise showed.

His room was different from the ones set aside for the Contiki tours. It had plush Berber carpets, velvet curtains matching the doona on his double bed, silver embossed wallpaper, and light wooden furnishings. He also had an ensuite; he didn't have to share a bathroom down the hallway.

'You have an ensuite?' Cara queried.

'Don't you?' David teased.

He answered the door, and the aroma of steaming coffee and pastries filled the room. Coffee was shared in bed, and Cara struggled to hold the blanket in place until David picked his shirt off the floor and said, 'The coffee will go cold if you don't put this on.'

As she took the shirt from him, the blanket slipped down to her waist; the coffee went cold.

Cara

After making love, tepid coffee and cold pastries were shared before showering. Cara, standing wrapped in a lavender-scented white fluffy towel, pulled the curtains back.

The moon hung close to the ground, creating ghostly shadows on the snow. Skiers carrying torches moved over the terrain, and the chair lift stood closed and silhouetted against the dark sky. Giant ants on an uphill march.

Cara didn't hear David return from the bathroom, and when he touched the scar on her shoulder she was thrown back into her past.

Cold, so cold, she was always cold. The dark wooden table was high and long, and there was never enough light. The sconce cast shadows around the room, reflecting off the man hanging on the cross on the dark walls. Her fingers slipped, and the plate she was putting on the table fell to the floor and shattered. Cara stood staring at the pieces, knowing what was going to happen.

'You are a useless, evil girl.' Grabbed by her pigtails and dragged into the dormitory, Cara felt the strap before it hit her.

She fell to the wooden floor crying, 'I'm sorry. I'm sorry.' Shrinking at her attacker's feet, she whimpered. 'No, no.'

Trying to protect herself, she flung her arms out, striking the perpetrator, but she was ten, and they were stronger than her.

Thrown across the room, Cara's shoulder smashed against the metal corner of a bed, ripping her body open. Paralysed with pain, she couldn't cry and struggled to breathe as blood covered the hard floor under her.

She tried to move, to lift her arms to protect herself as she cowered on the sticky floor, expecting another blow. The voice screamed at her. 'Useless, evil, child.'

Then, another voice. 'What are you doing! She is only a child.'

'She is evil.'

'She is a child.' Hands rested on her.

She cried, pushing them away, 'No, no, don't hurt me. I'm sorry.'

Cara thrashed at the hands on her shoulders as she writhed on the floor.

'Cara, I'm here. No one's going to hurt you … Cara, open your eyes. I've got you,' a gentle male voice said.

Cara opened her eyes. 'David?'

He knelt on the floor beside her, hands on her shoulders.

She was with David. 'David?'

He yanked the doona off the bed and wrapped it around them. 'I've got you, Cara; you're safe. I've got you.' She sank into his protective arms. 'I won't hurt you. I won't let anyone hurt you. You're here with me; you're safe.'

David wiped the tears from her face, and she dropped her head onto his chest and swallowed her sobs, trying to calm herself.

He eased her back, but she struggled against that, wanting to stay close to his heartbeat. He tightened his arms around her, stroking her hair. 'No one can hurt you. I've got you.'

His heartbeat thumped in her ear. Cara took short, sharp breaths, breathing with the rhythm. He tilted her chin and looked into her eyes. 'Will you tell me?'

Cara nodded, and the lie she'd told all her life hovered on her lips. The lie Tommy believed, the one she almost believed herself. She would not lie to David; would not say *I fell off my bike when I was little.*

David waited for her to speak. She was safe in his arms. He loved her, and she loved him. She could tell David the truth. She could tell him everything, but not now. Now, she sheltered in his arms, listening to his heartbeat, his naked body and the blanket wrapped around them, keeping her warm, away from the nightmare.

Now she said, 'Not all the Sisters were kind.'

David

David stared out the window. He'd sat on the floor with Cara in his arms until she quietened. The nightmare she was remembering faded, but a sadness surrounded her, and her strength seeped away until she fell asleep. He'd laid her in his bed and wrapped the blanket tightly around her.

He realised how little he knew about her, and he also knew by the burning in his chest and the wave of anger he struggled to control, he had made the right decision. No one would ever hurt Cara again.

He dressed and ordered more coffee. When Cara whimpered in her sleep, he sat on the bed and held her tightly until she settled.

No one would ever hurt Cara again.

Chapter Ten

Cara

Cara stood at the top of the ski run under a crisp blue sky. Sunshine would warm the day, but for now, her breath lingered in the air in front of her.

Today, the *Olympic Championships* for the Contiki Tour group would take place, and in two days, the tour bus would leave for London. David would meet her there.

A skier swished to a halt behind her. She turned, expecting David, but it was the blonde girl, Alice, who stood behind her.

Pushing her goggles onto her head, she said sweetly, 'Waiting for David?'

Cara nodded. She didn't want to talk to this woman.

The Contiki Tour group exited the chair lift and tramped across the snow to the top of the ski run. There was safety in that group. Cara didn't understand why that mattered. 'I have to go,' she said.

'Oh, don't go. You might want to hear what David has to say after his father's talked to him about you.' Alice flicked her hair behind her ears and smiled.

'David's father ....' *Why would David's father want to talk about me?*

'Oh, aren't you sweet?' Alice mocked. 'Didn't David tell you his father flew in this morning?'

David's sisters skied up beside Alice. She pulled her goggles over her eyes and said, 'Come on, let's get out of here.'

The girls glanced at each other. Indecision scattered over their faces, but they joined Alice as she skied away.

Cara clasped her hands together, keeping them still.

David's father.

She watched the girls ski down the slope, hair blowing out from under beanies, snow swirling around, skis and poles perfectly synchronised with their bodies. They were from a different world to her; everything about them screamed *different*.

Could she fit into that world? Was it one she wanted to fit into?

Jeremy seemed happy.

Cara clutched her skis and poles and went to join the tour group.

'Cara.' David skied to a stop in front of her. He pushed his goggles up. 'What did Alice want?'

'What did your father want?'

David's eyes tracked Alice as she skied away. 'I told him it's over with Alice, that I'm not getting back with her. I told him about you.'

'What did he say?'

'Alice always gets her way.' David shrugged his shoulders. 'I know it was foolish to think she understood, her father ...,' he left the rest unsaid. 'My father wants to meet you.'

To approve of me.

Like he'd read her mind, David said, 'No, Cara, to meet you.'

'I'm not like the girls you would normally bring home.'

'We are no different to you, Cara. We get up every day and go to work, just like you.'

'Not just like me,' Cara protested. 'I'm the girl behind the counter selling pots and pans, not the son of the store owner.'

'Come to dinner tomorrow and meet my father.'

'What about the *biggest retail empire*? How could your father approve of me if I mess that up.'

'It won't come to that. I'm not part of a business deal, to be married off to create a dynasty.'

He tried to make light of that. And when she protested, he took her in his arms and kissed her with coffee-flavoured lips, and all her fears flew away. 'It doesn't matter. I love you. We love each other. None of those things matter.'

But they did matter.

Cara pulled out of David's embrace, and he said, 'My father loves my mother, he will understand. I love you, and nothing will change that.'

'What about your mother?'

A smile filled David's eyes. 'She will understand.'

Her feet slipped on the snow-covered ground, and David put his arm around her. He tilted her chin, so she was looking into his eyes. Sunshine splashed across a muddy field, and her hands were stained with the sap of wild lilies. Maybe he was right—it was 1989, not 1889.

In his arms, it all seemed so simple.

'My parents will understand. I don't love Alice,' he said. 'I know that now; I should have known that before; I should have been more aware.'

He believed his parents would understand, and Cara knew then that he loved her enough to give his future away to be with her – to give his family away.

Could she let him?

'Come on, Cara,' Sharon shouted from the line of skiers waiting to begin the race. 'We are waiting for you.'

Cara turned to see Jeremy place a kiss on Sharon's cheek before he skied away.

'I'll meet you at the bottom,' David said.

Chapter Eleven

Cara

Cottesloe Beach was almost deserted when the last rays of an April sunset struck the ocean. Red and orange flames shot into the greying sky, white sands tinged red, and those fishing on the groyne shone like Christmas ornaments. The last of the bodyboarders left the water. Pulling off their flippers and tucking their boards under their arms, they trudged across the sand to shower before heading up to the car park.

Cara brushed sand from her bodyboard before plodding across the sand to her beach towel. Autumn was her favourite time of the year: the sun was still warm, the westerly winds blew softer and the swell had been good today. Soon, winter storms would wash away the sands and make bodyboarding unsafe, and she wouldn't be able to hide her emptiness in the ocean.

She sat on her beach towel, drying her hair, John Farnham's *Touch of Paradise* playing on the portable CD player beside her. She sang quietly along and looked out over the ocean.

She saw him, tall and slim. He flicked wet brown curls over his forehead as he came out of the water, surfboard under one arm. If she screwed her eyes up, she could be looking at David or Jeremy. He trudged towards a towel on the sand not far from her, shoved his surfboard upright into the sand, and peeled his Rip Curl wet suit down to his waist. Looking her way, he said, 'Excuse me, miss, do you know what time it is?'

Cara shook herself. He was nothing like David or Jeremy, but his accent broke her heart. 'Yes ... I'll check.' She rummaged around in her bag and took her wristwatch out. By the setting sun, she thought it was about 5:30, and she was right. 'Five-thirty.'

'Thanks.' The man picked up his beach towel and wrapped it around his shoulders. 'Did you catch some good waves?'

Cara looked out over the ocean as the sun melted into the horizon, leaving gold slashes splattering the water. 'Yes.'

'It's really good here.'

'Are you on holiday?' she asked.

'Sort of.' He rubbed his hair with a towel. 'Do you live nearby?'

'Not far.' Cara pulled a Billabong jumper out of her beach bag. John Farnham was now singing *You're the Voice,* and she switched the buttons off, peeled her wetsuit top down and pulled her jumper over her wet swimsuit and shivered. *It's getting cold. And it will be dark soon.*

'Nice talking to you.' He picked his board up, and Cara watched him walk away across the beach. He stopped at a shower and washed the sand off his board before slogging up the curving road to the car park.

Cara pushed herself off the sand, rolled her wet towel into a ball, tossed it into her beach bag, and put her CD player on top.

It was time to go. Liz still made a fuss if she was home late.

The girls were sharing a two-room flat near Cottesloe Beach while Cara helped Liz arrange her wedding to Mike in June. Every morning she woke and pretended, put a smile on her face and kept her secrets. She was tired, the secrets and lies wearing her down. How she wanted to tell someone the truth, but the cost was too high for David.

She'd left him sleeping in Austria the last time they'd made love when he vowed he would stay with her forever, and she knew he would. They'd made plans to meet in London. 'I must stay with Sarah and Elyse,' he'd said. 'I promised my parents I would keep them safe and show them all the sights. We will return to London at the end of February, then I can be with you, we will be together.'

Being careful not to wake him, Cara dressed and hurried to the room she shared with her friends. She wasn't going back to London. She loved David too much to ask him to choose between her and his family. She was going home, away from the cold and wet, back to the sunshine she loved, and she wanted to be alone, not having to pretend everything was alright.

Her heart had been in pieces; nothing had ever hurt this much, but she was determined. She could not let David lose his future, his family – she couldn't let him do that for *a little tramp he'd met on holiday*. He didn't know what being without a family meant; she did.

Cara had grabbed her backpack from under her bed, put in what she could find, and left two notes – one for her friends, telling them she was going home and not to worry, and one for David.

She scribbled and scrunched up several lots of paper before she wrote,

> *My Darling David,*
>
> *I'm sorry. I know you believe your parents will accept me, and maybe they might, but if you lost your family over me, it would be more than I could bear. Our worlds are so far apart, let me keep a memory of you and a holiday promise.*
>
> *I will never forget you. I love you, but I will not destroy your life.*
>
> *Forgive me.*
>
> *Cara-Rose*

Taking a taxi to Saint Johann and a bus to Vienna that evening, she'd caught a train to London, packed a suitcase, withdrew her savings from the bank, and booked a ticket on a Qantas Jet before the tour got back to London. This way she avoided having to explain anything.

Three days later, she stood at the door of a building she'd called home. Three weeks later, in the middle of February, Liz, who'd come home to be with Mike, stood at that door telling her she couldn't explain to David what she didn't know.

'I didn't know how much you wanted him to know. I told him I would give you this.' She handed Cara a letter.

Darling Cara-Rose,

Understand how I love you. When you threw that snowball in my direction, you struck me over the heart, and my world changed forever. I'm sure we knew when we looked into each other's eyes that our lives were never going to be the same. I love you and want a life with you, nothing will change that.

When my sisters' trip is over, my life will be my own. Let me spend that life with you.

My parents will not make me choose between you and them, but if they do, I will choose you and make a family with you. Let me keep my promises to you for more than a holiday.

I love you and always will.

David

That was six weeks ago. She'd replied but didn't post the letter. She knew David loved her and would keep his word. He would choose between his family and her. He would give up his family for her. She could not let him do that, she would live without him, and he would return to his life. That was the only way it could be. That was the decision she'd made.

There were times she thought she'd put David out of her mind. But then she'd see someone who had a look of him about them, hear an American accent in the store, or see lovers walking along the beach. Memories would overwhelm her. She would be back in Austria, sitting on the floor, David's arms wrapped around her, where she knew she was safe. She had only ever trusted one other person in her life; he was the only person she'd felt safe with, until that day. That was the day she knew she could tell David everything.

Now, she put David into the cupboard in her head, with all her other secrets, so they couldn't hurt her. That way, she would survive.

***

The iron in Cara's hand crawled across a pair of blue denim jeans as she watched the six o'clock news on an old black and white television. The encounter with a stranger on the beach last week still bothered her.

Police are trying to identify an injured man found on the streets of Fremantle. He is 6ft 3 in tall, has curly brown hair and a slim build. Anyone with information, please call 124356, the newscaster announced as an identikit picture flashed on the screen.

'Liz, Liz!' Cara cried, her heart racing. Liz came rushing into the living room. 'Liz, it's David.' Cara pointed at the screen.

The picture stayed on the screen a few seconds longer, *anyone with any information is urged to contact their local police station or call 124356.*

'Liz.' Cara crumbled, tears falling down her cheeks.

The material on her jeans began to scorch, the smell filling the apartment. Liz grabbed the iron and set it on the end of the ironing board before she took Cara by the arms. 'It could be anyone.'

'No, Liz, no, it's David.'

Chapter Twelve

Cara

Cara sat beside a bed in the hospital ward staring at the bruised and swollen face. His eyes were closed; he seemed to be asleep but a machine kept him breathing.

In and out.

In and out.

She could hear his heartbeat on the monitor– and see a line recording the movement.

Up and down.

Up and down.

With Cara in distress, Liz had called Mike, and after calling the local police station, they'd raced down Stirling Highway. By the time Cara reached Royal Perth Hospital reception, her legs were shaking so much she couldn't walk. Mike held her upright as she stuttered and stumbled over her words, trying to explain who she was, trying to get permission to see David. Only family and only one visitor per patient.

Only family. She wasn't family.

Cara struggled with her words; she didn't want to make a fuss; she didn't see the police officer as he stood beside her and obtained permission for her to see David. Letting him take her arm, he guided her into the intensive care ward cubicle.

Now she sat holding a hand, but it wasn't David's hand. It was Jeremy's. Fingers moved in her hand. 'Cara.' Jeremy opened his eyes, struggling to talk through the mask that helped him breathe. He fixed his eyes on her.

'I'm here.' Cara leaned closer.

'I'm sorry …,' Jeremy mumbled. He looked past her into the distance, then turned his eyes back to her. 'Where's Sharon?'

'Still in London.' Sharon was still in London, hoping for her big break.

'No, she can't be.' Jeremy strained to sit in the bed. 'I've got to see her.' He pulled at the breathing mask, sweat covering his brow. The machines keeping him alive screamed, piercing the silence. Nursing staff ran into the room.

Jeremy thrashed around the bed, and an injection pushed into his thigh gradually calmed him.

Cara picked up his limp hand and whispered, 'Jeremy.'

Medical staff checked the machines, and one said, 'He's sleeping, let him rest.'

Cara turned to the speaker, a young woman about her age dressed in blue with a stethoscope around her neck. She wrote on the notes at the bottom of the bed and checked all the readings from the machines.

'What happened to Jeremy?' Cara asked. 'The police didn't say much.'

'We are not sure, it looks like a hit and run.'

'No one stopped?'

'Not the car that hit him,' the young woman said as she looked up from her notes. 'Passers-by found him and saved his life.'

Cara shook her head; she'd been sure the image on the television was David. *Why was Jeremy here? What had happened?*

***

Cara spent that night sitting in a chair. Her back ached, and she had a crick in her neck, but she was not leaving Jeremy alone. During the night, the large breathing machine was turned off, and he breathed with the help of a small face mask.

He lay unmoving, the swelling around his eyes seeming less pronounced, but it was hard to tell with his face so swollen. He had not woken again.

Cara sat watching and waiting as medical staff came and went. The police officer she'd seen the day before, questioned her. 'What is his name? Do you know where he lives? His family? What can you tell me about him?'

All Cara knew was his name. 'Jeremy Stonehouse. His father owes a store in Milwaukee.'

'A US citizen?'

Cara guessed so. And what more did she know about him? She knew nothing more about him other than that he was kind and gentle. *Why would anyone leave him like this?*

Liz and Mike dragged Cara home that night and made her eat and sleep at home before driving her back to the hospital the next day.

Cara turned as the young woman she'd seen earlier entered the cubical. She took the hand Cara held and felt for the pulse, looked at the machines and wrote notes on the clipboard at the end of the bed.

'Will he be alright?' Cara held back her tears.

'We won't know until he wakes up. But he's breathing on his own now, and that's a good sign.' The young woman, either a doctor or a nurse, comforted Cara.

'Cara.' Jeremy's eyes had opened again, and he was looking at her.

'I'm here.' She brushed the hair from his eyes and took his hand.

'I have to find Sharon,' he mumbled.

'When you're better,' Cara promised, caressing his fingers. 'We will find her when you're better.'

Jeremy closed his eyes. She thought he would sleep, but he jolted awake and tried to sit. 'The letter ...,' he cried.

'We'll worry about that later.' The young woman spoke firmly and placed her hand gently on Jeremy's chest. 'You need to rest.'

When he was asleep, she said to Cara, 'Come outside.'

Cara followed her out into the corridor. It was stuffy and busy with medical staff rushing back and forth. The smell of antiseptic couldn't cover the smell of disease and injury. They sat on cream-coloured plastic chairs as patients on beds and wheelchairs rolled along the corridor. Doctors and nurses hurried about and visitors scurried around.

The tea trolley stopped in front of them. Cara took the tea offered and held the cup in two hands to keep it steady.

'Are you family?' Cara was asked. She swept her fingers across her cheeks, shrugged her shoulders and shook her head. 'I didn't know Jeremy was here until I saw the news.'

'And Sharon?'

'No, she's not family either.' Cara didn't know what to say. She'd seen Jeremy kiss Sharon, but what more did she know? She might guess what Jeremy wanted to talk to Sharon about.

They'd argued before. 'I can't get pregnant,' Sharon yelled. 'I'm on the pill.'

'Getting pregnant is not the worst thing that can happen; make sure you use a condom.' *Use a condom!* Sometimes, she wished Sharon would grow up.

Surely, they would have used a condom.

Still, Cara remembered the lessons from school. The only way to be one hundred per cent sure was to abstain.

***

Cold sand squished through Cara's toes as she walked along Cottesloe Beach. Sneakers in one hand, she wrapped her arms around herself, trying to keep warm. She'd left Jeremy sleeping in the hospital, taken the advice given and gone home, but she didn't go home – she went to the beach to think.

'Hi.'

Cara looked up; she hadn't been paying attention and stumbled into his path. 'Sorry.'

'Not surfing today?' He flicked his wet hair out of his eyes. *Who are you?*

'No, a bit cold today. Did you get some good waves?'

'Is everything okay?' he asked.

Cara stared, just a surfer on holiday, enjoying the last autumn waves. No one she knew, no one who knew her. 'Yes, everything is alright.'

But it wasn't. Jeremy was in the hospital; Sharon hadn't come home, and Jeremy needed to see her. Sharon hadn't said anything about Jeremy in her last letter.

He rubbed his wet hair and said, 'Maybe I'll see you tomorrow.'

'Yes.'

Cara watched him leave the beach. When he turned and waved to her from the carpark, she returned his wave. Then she realised how cold it was; it was time to go home.

Chapter Thirteen

Cara

Cara sat opposite Jeremy in the hospital café, staring at the paper in her hand, pushing back the tears that came too easily.

Jeremy reached across the table and held her hand, 'I'm sorry.'

Cara lifted her chin. 'No, it's okay.'

She stared out the window of the café, which sat on a bridge overlooking the roadway with cars rushing underneath.

David had written:

> *Dear Cara-Rose,*
>
> *I am sorry. I want to let you know that Alice told me she is pregnant, and we are to marry at the end of March. I will make a life for Alice and my child. I know you understand; you are right; life is not simple, and I promise to do the best for my child.*
>
> *I hope you can forgive me for my broken promises. I will always cherish my memory of you and my time in Austria with you.*
>
> *David*

'March,' Cara muttered. It was almost the end of April.

'He didn't know where to find you, Cara. He wrote the letter hoping he could get it to you. No one left any addresses. He sent someone to look for you. He wanted you to know he didn't abandon you.'

The surfer on the beach?

'Was it a nice wedding?' Cara didn't know what else to say.

'Yes. Alice was happy and looked lovely, the girls looked lovely.' Jeremy paused as if unsure about what to say next. 'And the family seemed happy; everyone seemed happy.'

'David?' Cara murmured.

'He will do what is expected of him.'

Expected of him.

Cara breathed deeply. 'David will make a good family for his child.' She knew that.

Jeremy held her hand, and she looked into his eyes. He was recovering, the injuries to his face fading; he had use of his arms and upper body, but he was unable to use his legs.

'How are you?' Cara asked.

Jeremy looked away and took a deep breath. 'Some days are better than others. The doctors are hopeful I'll recover; *it's early days, and it takes time,* they tell me.' He chewed his bottom lip. 'I've got to find Sharon; I'm sure you know why.'

Cara nodded.

'I gave her my address, but she didn't give me hers. She wrote to me and told me she was pregnant, that she didn't know what to do with the baby. It wasn't what she had planned, and she was going back to Australia. When David found your address, I came searching for Sharon. I'm hoping you know where she is?'

'Jeremy, I'm … she is still in London; she didn't say anything about a baby in her last letter. Her mother went back to London to her husband, and she is staying with them.'

'London's too far?' Jeremy uttered. 'Do you think she will talk to me? Is it too late … I can't fly.'

'We can try. I have the phone number. Sharon's a good girl, sometimes she does stupid things, but I'm sure she won't ….' Cara couldn't be sure, though; she knew how important the *big break* was for Sharon.

The next day, Cara stood beside Jeremy as he argued over the phone with Sharon. She could hear his desperate pleas. She could not hear what Sharon said.

Jeremy wiped his tears away when he hung up the phone.

Chapter Fourteen

Cara

Sharon came home for Liz and Mike's wedding in June, trying to hide her pregnancy. She made Cara swear not to tell Jeremy, who had returned to the USA, that she was keeping his baby.

After the wedding, Cara and Sharon shared the apartment in Cottesloe. Jennifer was born on 15th October 1989, and she looked like her father. Cara's heart broke. Jeremy should know about his daughter, but Sharon had made her promise.

The hot summer was full of sleepless nights and days spent watching Jennifer grow and keeping the truth hidden from Jeremy. Cara knew how to hide the truth.

When Jennifer was six months old, Sharon and Cara argued. Hiding the truth from Jeremy was bruising her soul – how many more lies did she need to live with?

'Jennifer is *my* daughter, not yours,' Sharon snapped.

They were sitting at the table in the kitchen of the little flat in Cottesloe.

'She is also Jeremy's daughter.'

'Jeremy – Jeremy. You should have fallen for Jeremy instead of moping around after someone way out of your league.' Sharon's ugly words crushed Cara. She stared across the table, tears stinging her eyes.

'He's married, Cara, he has a family of his own, and I have my daughter.' Sharon never knew when to stop. 'Get your own family.'

Cara had argued with Sharon before, but this was different; this tore her apart. She knew she shouldn't let those tears fall, but they did. .

Her face must have shown the anguish for Sharon scraped her chair, pushed it back and hurried around the table. 'I'm sorry. I didn't mean that.' She put her arms around Cara. And for the first time since she'd known Sharon, Cara wanted to be anywhere except in this room with Sharon's arms around her, but she said, 'It's okay.'

In June, Sharon started part-time modelling, and with government support money and a generous landlord, Cara knew her friend could afford the rent on the flat in Cottesloe. It was time to move. She loved Jennifer like her own, but she was *not* her child, and Sharon's words hurt more than she thought possible. She had added another lie to her life.

Cara began looking for an apartment, and when she saw a For Sale notice in the paper, she made an offer to purchase. Selling her car and scrambling enough money together for a deposit, Cara applied for a loan. Even though interest rates were extraordinarily high at 17-18%, she found a bank manager who didn't take her gender into account and looked only at her ability to meet the payments, and she bought the little apartment.

The apartment was old, the building dating back to the 1930s, and it needed refurbishing, but it had two bedrooms and was in the city with easy access to Cara's work. She painted the internal brick walls white; the fixtures and fittings had been renovated in the 70s and needed updating, but they were serviceable. The orange bench tops with brown cupboards and the purple and white bathroom had a certain charm. Cara filled the apartment with furniture from secondhand shops, except for the beds and linen, which she bought brand new. From the balcony, she could see across the grass of Langley Park to the Swan River. She could see the hills in the distance to the east, and at night, the South

Perth foreshore twinkled with lights.

She received a letter from Jeremy each month, and each month she kept Jeremy's daughter a secret from him.

Chapter Fifteen

David

On a cold March evening in 1991, David Hayle opened the front door to his home, his child's cries filling the air. He dropped his bag on the floor and ripped his jacket off as he raced across the foyer and up the wooden staircase. Slamming the nursery door open, he found his son thrashing about in his crib.

David lifted the distressed child as gently as he could from the crib, held him close and patted his back, soothing the anguish. 'Shush, shush, I'm here. I've got you. Daddy's here.'

The child's body heaved, his sobs coming in long wails.

'You're home?' The question was more of an accusation.

David concentrated on the crying child. 'Shhh, Shhh.' The child's sobs lessened. He was dirty, his diaper soaked, and the wet seeped through to David's chest.

'Where's Nancy?'

'I sent her home. She's a sneak … your little spy keeping an eye on me.'

He comforted his child as turned to face his wife. 'She's here to help you.' Then he turned his back, took the child to the changing table, and wiped his tear-stained face before changing him, all the while soothing him.

'Change his bed,' he said as he left the nursery.

He carried the child down the stairs into the kitchen, warmed a bottle and sat on the couch holding and soothing him while he fed.

I'm sorry, little man, I'm sorry; it shouldn't be like this.

The college drinking parties that had seemed so much fun when they were teenagers and young adults he'd grown out of. Alice had not, and it had taken him too long to notice.

This wasn't the first time he'd come home to find Brandon crying in his crib. The first time Alice had been asleep on the couch. That was when he understood.

Alice had seemed resentful at being pregnant with Brandon. At first, he wondered if it was grief over their first baby's death – it had happened so soon after they married – and they had cried in each other's arms. When Alice told him she was pregnant again, he attended doctors' appointments and scans with her, and it seemed to bring them closer.

But he understood the resentment now. Alice had stopped drinking. She did that for Brandon, but she hadn't stopped drinking when she was pregnant with their first baby, and sometimes, he wondered, but he never went there.

When he suggested Alice speak to someone, she screamed at him, 'There is nothing wrong with me! I drink when I want to.'

She'd hit him that day, lunging across the room, striking him with her fists and scratching his face. The only way he could protect himself was to restrain her, so he'd turned his back and walked away.

His child fell asleep as he emptied the bottle, so David carried him back to his room. The house was cold, and the heating was off. But the bed was clean, the linen changed, and the dirty laundry no longer in the room. David laid the child in his crib, wrapped him warmly in a blanket, turned the room's heating on low, and went to shower.

He stepped from the shower onto the warm Italian ceramic tiles and pulled a towel from the heated rack as the door opened.

'Is he asleep?' Alice asked him.

'Yes.'

'I'm sorry.' She stood in the doorway. Through the steam, he could see her dishevelled hair and her crumbled clothing, and he could smell alcohol.

'You are always sorry.'

'You were late home, it's not … .'

'Go to bed, Alice. We'll talk about it tomorrow.'

She stepped towards him, and he flinched, stepping away from her. He could not do this now. She turned away and he locked the bathroom door behind her.

He dressed in his pyjamas and his old-fashioned red and blue checked woollen dressing gown, just like Grandad. He looked in on Alice. They no longer shared a bedroom, had not shared a bedroom for more than six months. When Brandon moved into the nursery, Alice told David she wanted their bedroom to herself. He did not object.

Alice was strewn across the bed still clothed. He pulled a blanket over her, turned the heating low, and shut the door. They would talk about it tomorrow like they always did, and they would fight. She would argue that she had no problem with drink, but he saw it differently. That is why he'd hired Nancy, not for Alice but for Brandon.

He kept their lives a secret, displaying a happy family and a safe home for Brandon to grow. He was busy at work, the merger in April a month away, and Alice's father expected him to play a key role in the new store. They presented the façade of a perfect, professional young family, attending social functions and living in a house they had renovated in Pacific Heights.

Brandon's grandparents doted on him, especially David's father, who now had an heir to continue the family name. David had argued with his father: 'It's the 90s, Dad, you've got three children and two grandchildren. Sarah's son has as much of your blood in him as Brandon.' It did not make any difference.

Sometimes, he wanted to end the pretence and tell the truth, but he kept it hidden. It was too late to have a life of his own, but he would make sure Brandon did.

In the nursery, David pulled the white rocking chair close to the crib and checked his son's breathing. It was quiet and steady. He leaned back on the chair and closed his eyes.

His thoughts took him back to the dinner party in London, the Ritz Hotel. Gold-rimmed China sat on a white tablecloth in a room with red and blue Egyptian carpet and golden wall lamps – Elyse's 21st birthday. Alice had joined the celebration from Milan, dressed in designer clothes, with flawless makeup and hair. She had taken his arm, sitting beside him, talking and enjoying their meal, and he thought they might be friends.

After the birthday candles and the song-singing, when dessert was served, Alice stood, tapped her glass, and announced. 'David and I have some wonderful news.' She'd paused for effect and looked down at him adoringly. 'We are expecting a baby in August.'

There was a quiet gasp and then a burst of excitement following the announcement. Looking around, his mother's eyes met his across the table. He put a smile on his face, stood and embraced Alice.

The wedding took place at the end of March, *the one every little girl dreamed of. He'd been the groom and then the husband.*

Cara floated into his mind, and he pushed her away. Some days, it was hard to push her away, but she could not be there. He had a son to bring up.

The child stirred in his cot and murmured in his sleep; David placed his hand on his back.

'I'm here,' he whispered to the sleeping child. 'I'll always be here.'

***

The next morning, David sat at the breakfast table in the kitchen with Brandon in his highchair. Alice came bouncing down the stairs, dressed in her gym clothes, her blonde hair pulled back tight in a ponytail, her make-up perfect. There was no sign of yesterday on her face unless you looked closely.

Alice was stunning; she was one of the most beautiful women he knew. They were the King and Queen of the Prom in High School, the golden couple, expected to achieve whatever they desired.

'Come for a run with mummy?' she said to Brandon.

David wanted to shout, '*You are not taking him.*'

Brandon wasn't yet one year old, a baby too young to remember what happened yesterday. He reached his arms up to his mother. She picked him out of his chair and snuggled into his hair, holding him tight. Alice loved Brandon, but it wasn't enough to stop her from drinking and leaving him crying in his crib. If he tried to talk to her, they would scream and shout, and she would hit out at him.

'There's coffee in the pot,' he said.

Putting Brandon back into his highchair, Alice ruffled the child's hair before she poured herself coffee and sat opposite David.

Everything looked perfect. Spring sunshine came through the kitchen windows. Italian marble benchtops sat on white kitchen cupboards, wooden chairs scattered around the oak kitchen table, and green plants hung from pots in the windows. Coffee percolating filled the room with aroma, and pastries sat on the table. Brandon chewed on toast and tried to take spoons of cereal from a bowl.

Perfect!

'Don't send Nancy home until I get home in future,' he said.

'Why? I can mind my little boy. I don't need her help.'

Alice looked over the top of her coffee cup, and he wondered if she didn't remember what happened yesterday. He'd never been so drunk he couldn't remember what he'd done the next day.

'Don't you remember...'

'Of course, I remember, you were late home.' She scowled at him. 'It's not my fault if you are late home.'

'Brandon was crying ... Nancy would have ....'

'I'm his mother.' Alice argued. 'Not her.'

Her voice was beginning to rise, and he said, 'Go for your run. I'll mind Brandon.'

'He can come.' Alice thumped her coffee cup onto the table and pushed herself from the chair. Then he saw the shake in her hands as she leaned against the table; she noticed it and noticed him seeing it. She looked him in the eyes, and for a moment, he thought they might talk, but she turned away from him and went to take Brandon from the highchair.

David's chair screeched along the tiles as he pushed it back, scooping the little boy out of the highchair and holding him close. 'Go for your run.'

Chapter Sixteen

Cara

It was 1991, and the beginning of spring in Perth, Western Australia. Cara stood beside the kitchen table, reading words she could not understand. She did not hear the key in the door, and her tear-stained face looked up as Jeremy came through the doorway.

'Hey?' he queried.

'Sharon's ....'

Cara handed him a letter dated 21st August 1991.

> *My dear Cara,*
>
> *I am sorry to tell you that our darling Sharon has passed away. I do not know what she has told you. For the last few months, Sharon had been suffering from what appeared to be severe flu, and then she contracted sepsis which the doctors were unable to control. She believed she would recover and return to Australia, to you and her little girl, my granddaughter, who I never knew existed and who I hope to meet one day.*
>
> *She told me the child's father doesn't know of her but that you believe he would want to be involved in her life. I hope this is so and he and you will include me in Jennifer's life.*
>
> *I am sorry, I don't know what else to tell you. As her dreams became harder to reach, Sharon became*

rash and didn't take care of herself. She will always be in my heart, and I am sure in yours as well.

I have included a letter addressed to you that I found in Sharon's personal effects. There is also an envelope addressed to Jeremy.

Marion.

Cara stumbled across the room and collapsed onto the blue floral settee. She stared dumbly at the paper in Jeremy's hands as he read the letter. He pushed his wheelchair over to the settee and heaved himself out of it to sit beside her.

'Sharon ....' Her words caught in her throat. She hadn't expected this ... why had she been kept in the dark? 'What ... why didn't she ...?'

And the memories flooded back, all those years ago. Two four-year-olds meeting for the first time, when they said goodbye, when they said hello again, the good days, the bad days, the arguments, the making up, the last argument.

'Why didn't she tell me?'

Sharon had been away for over four months. She'd taken a modelling contract in London and asked Cara to mind Jennifer. 'I can't take a child with me, it's London. It's only a month. My parents don't know about her. They won't understand. Will you mind Jennifer?'

Sharon hadn't been back in a month; she hadn't answered phone calls or letters or been in touch with Cara since she left Perth in April.

After four months with no contact, Cara would no longer keep Sharon's secret from Jeremy, and he rushed to Perth to meet his daughter.

Jeremy put his arms around Cara, and she turned her face into his chest and sobbed until she ran out of tears.

'My poor girl,' she mumbled.

Cara pushed herself out of Jeremy's arms, forced herself from the settee, walked down the hallway to a bedroom, and opened the door to look in on the sleeping child. Jennifer had tossed her blankets onto the floor and Cara picked them up and tucked them around the little girl before bending and kissing her forehead.

'I'm here,' she whispered. 'I'll always be here.'

Cara turned to find Jeremy at the door. She knew he would have made a home and family for Sharon and their daughter if she'd let him.

'I'm sorry, Jeremy,' she said, wiping the tears from his face.

***

In the kitchen, Cara filled the kettle and made tea, and placed the pot and cups on the wooden coffee table in front of the settee.

A cup of tea will fix everything, Cara remembered Elizabeth's mother saying the day she moved into their home.

Sometimes, we could use something stronger.

'I don't have anything stronger,' Cara said.

'Tea's good.' Jeremy poured the tea, and memories of happy days wafted in the tannins that filled the air of the little apartment. He was right, *tea was good*. He opened the envelope addressed to him and showed it to Cara. It held a note with three words on it: *I am sorry*. It also had Jennifer's birth certificate and a statutory declaration that Jeremy was Jennifer's father.

Cara's fingers fumbled with the envelope addressed to her. Sharon had written:

My dear Cara,

I know I should have told you I was unwell earlier. I should have been more careful, and I have let you and Jennifer down. I know you are looking after my precious girl for me, and I hope Jeremy still wants to be involved in her life. I should have told him about her, I am so sorry about that. Please make sure he knows about Jennifer. I am sorry I made you promise to keep her a secret from him. I hope you both can forgive me.

I have tried to keep the identity of this sickness from my mother, you know how difficult she is, and the symptoms are like flu, so that is what I have. It's a strange thing, some days I am fine, but they don't last. I have been offered a trial with some experimental drugs; these have proved successful at slowing this disease and should give me more time to spend with you and Jennifer. I will let you know as soon as the trial finishes, and I can travel back home to you. I miss my little girl, and I miss you, my dearest friend.

Shaz xxx

The letter was dated 5th August 1991.

Chapter Seventeen

David

David opened the door to his home; it was warm and quiet, as he expected. At not quite thirty years old, his position in upper management was much whispered about, *the manager's son-in-law*. It had become his and Alice's responsibility to arrange the Christmas party for junior management and the store's staff.

1991 had been a successful year. Alice had convinced her father that the time was right to add an Italian Fashion House to the store, even though the economy was still struggling, and more people were opting to spend their wages in cut-price department stores.

Alice had been right, and she worked for the designer on the 1st floor of the store, wearing his clothing and encouraging her friends and acquaintances to spend their money.

She maintained her perfect look and impeccable dress, but he wondered for how long. She was the General Manager's daughter, and any indiscretions were discreetly ignored.

Alice spent an extraordinary amount of money on the Christmas party, saying the staff should be thanked. The party was held in the store on the upper level, under the glass dome. Food and drink were provided, and a local band, *Olive Generation*, provided the entertainment.

Alice wore a Versace black silk and velvet three-quarter-length gown with a round neck and long sleeves, split up to the thigh, the opening held together with laces. It clung to her perfectly sculptured body, her blonde hair curled and bundled on top of her head, and her makeup flawless. He dressed in a Navy-blue Versace evening suit, white shirt, and blue tie, and they were *the Golden Couple.*

Alice was happy she spent the evening flirting and dancing, and David was happy and proud of her. He wanted this time, this life, to last for Alice and himself, to be happy for her.

As they walked across the wooden foyer of their home, Alice stumbled on her Manolo Blahnik high heels, and he put his arm around her to steady her. She turned to him and put her arms around his neck, seeking his mouth. He gently pulled her arms away; they had not had sex since he moved out of their bedroom. That was Alice's choice, and this was his.

Alice stepped back, glaring at him. 'Are you still thinking about that little whore from Austria?'

She'd been drinking – no more than many people at the party – it was a celebration after all, but he didn't want to do this. 'Don't, Alice, don't do this.'

'Why not? That little whore is still in your head, isn't she?' she snarled.

He went to walk past her to go upstairs to his room, but she grabbed his arm. 'You're mine, David, not hers.'

He shrugged her hands off and walked away, but she called after him, 'Poor David, so honourable, always doing the right thing.' Her voice rose. 'Poor David, so easy to manipulate.'

He reeled. The air left him. His legs stopped working. He couldn't move. He had never doubted Alice, never questioned her when she told him she was pregnant. David turned slowly to face Alice and saw contempt and scorn in her eyes. He saw the truth.

So easy to manipulate.

He had grieved for a child that had not existed.

'Always doing the right thing,' Alice slung the words at him, pushed past him and staggered up the stairs.

At the top of the staircase, his mother rocked Brandon in her arms as Alice lurched past them.

So easy to manipulate.

***

Five weeks later, at the end of January 1992, after Christmas celebrations with his parents, grandparents and extended family, after a New Year's celebration spent with Alice's parents on the snow at Saint Moritz, he sat at the breakfast table across from Alice and said, 'You don't love me, Alice. Maybe you did once, or was it always control – I don't know any more and I don't care.'

And that surprised him because he didn't care – once, he would have worried about hurting her, about what people would think.

'You lied to me – let me grieve. I don't understand that, but none of it matters now. I'm leaving. You can have the house and whatever you want. I won't fight you for anything.'

Alice flicked her hair back and smirked at him across the table, 'You will not see Brandon.'

He wasn't surprised by her reaction. He sipped his coffee as he looked out the window. The green leaves on the trees glistened with rain, and little red and grey birds hopped around. Simple and free. Cara had said *life's not like that, David.* Now he knew.

'I will fight you for Brandon; you can't stop me from seeing him. I've done nothing a court would consider allowing that.'

'Oh, but David, you have.' Alice smiled sweetly at him. 'I'm sure the courts would love to hear about the little whore from Austria.'

'I haven't seen Cara since we got married.'

'Will they believe that?'

He struggled to keep calm. He wanted to slam his cup down on the table. Instead, he placed it gently and said, 'I'm sure the courts would love to hear about me coming home and finding Brandon screaming if you are going to go there.'

'I'm a young mother, I get tired; you shouldn't be home late all the time. What are you doing late at work all the time, talking to the whore?' Alice brushed her hair back and tilted her head, a sad smile on her face. Her voice was soft and trembling as she wiped her cheeks, and he saw how she would manipulate and control the truth.

'Cara has nothing to do with this. Leave her out of it.'

'Oh, I can't do that. I'm sure the courts will want to know everything about her, and they will see you are unfit to be in Brandon's life. I will make sure of that,' she hissed.

Chapter Eighteen

David

In August 1992, David Hayle stood beside a grave. A gentle breeze moved the leaves of an old gum tree that provided shade as magpies warbled from its branches. He watched the coffin lowered, listened to the prayers offered, and tried to keep his mind on where he was.

He had not expected to see Cara standing on the other side of the grave, dressed in black, tears on her face, her golden curls moving in the wind. Her eyes met his as she picked up sand and let it fall into the grave before moving away. David held his grandmother's arm as she scattered sand over the coffin. The priest said his final prayers, cast sand into the grave, and then the funeral party moved away.

David helped his grandmother to the waiting car, and his grandfather and mother joined her.

'I'll be along in a minute; don't wait for me,' he said, not wanting or needing to explain.

Cara sat on a bench under a tree, the late morning sun warming the air. She dabbed her eyes and wiped her face.

'Hi,' David said as he sat beside her.

'Hi.' Cara's eyes, her emerald eyes, misty with tears, looked into his. He wanted to put his arms around her and hold her tight, but he could not.

'How are you here?' Cara asked.

He could see her trying to keep her voice calm and steady. 'Frank Kelly is a close friend of my grandparents, my mother's uncle. And you?'

'Father Kelly was kind to me. He was a good man, what a religious person should be.' Cara wiped her tears away. The wind blew ruby curls across her tear-stained face, and he could not stop himself. He pushed them away from her eyes, her beautiful, tear-filled eyes. He felt her tremble at his touch, all the promises he'd made, the promises he'd broken.

'I'm sorry,' he said. There was much he wanted to tell her, and he hoped she would allow him to do that.

'No, David, … I understand.'

'Will you come back to the house for the farewell?'

Cara hesitated, and he was afraid she would say no, but then she said, 'I would like that.'

In the front room of a renovated house on Bellevue Street, Fremantle, David's family gathered with friends from the church. Drinks and food were served, and speeches made.

David saw Cara trying to move; he saw the hand on Cara's arm restricting her movement. He remembered holding Cara in his arms on the floor in a hotel in Austria and Cara saying, 'Not all the Sisters were kind.' He remembered the anger and the uselessness of that anger.

He made his way through the crowd until he stood before her. 'Is everything okay?' he asked.

'This is none of your concern, young man,' a woman in a long black dress told him.

'Everything is okay,' Cara told him, but he knew she wasn't telling him the truth. The woman released her grip, and Cara fled.

Cara

Sitting on the swing hanging from the thick branches of an old gum tree, Cara turned her face to the warm winter sunshine.

She pushed sand around with her feet. Sister Camille's fury at her for attending the funeral had sapped her. Would she ever be free of it? Cara would always be poison in the eyes of Sister Camille, and those who thought like her, but Father Kelly was kind; he hadn't treated her like that. She wanted to say goodbye.

'Did you know Father Kelly well?'

Cara's nerves leapt and she turned to the speaker, a tall, slim blonde-haired woman, about in her mid-forties. It was a gentle enquiry and the woman's hazel eyes looked kind.

'He was kind to me when I was young. I will miss him.'

'Yes,' she said. 'He was a special man.'

Cara nodded.

'Are you alright? I saw that Nun with you?'

'Yes. Some of them are not very nice.'

'I know.'

'Emmaline,' a voice called from the steps.

Cara saw a dark-haired man cross the lawn. He put his arms around the woman, and Cara didn't need words to know how much they loved each other.

'Father Kelly was kind to ....' The woman looked at Cara.

'Cara.'

'Father Kelly helped Cara when she was young.'

'Like he helped you,' the man said.

The woman, Emmaline, nodded and wiped her tears away.

The back door opened, and David sat on the top step, staring over the lawn to where she sat, his eyes on her.

Cara sensed the couple exchange glances.

'We should go inside,' Emmaline said.

As the couple walked past David, the man placed his hand on David's shoulder.

Cara pushed herself off the swing and climbed the steps to join him. She didn't know why she'd said yes to coming to the house .. to see him again? Was that enough? She wiped her eyes, sucked in air, and chewed absently on her fingers. She was foolish to think seeing him could be enough, but it had to be.

'I shouldn't have come.'

'Yes, you should.'

'Perhaps…'

'Daddy,' a little voice called.

Cara turned to see David's son, just over two, running across the veranda. The child threw himself into David's arms, and he held him close and tussled his blond hair.

Cara knew it could not be any other way.

'Cara,' Jeremy said from the veranda behind her. She stood and wrapped her arms around him before standing back from the wheelchair to look at him.

'I'm good,' he said before she could ask. Cara took his hand. He had recovered from his injuries, but some days, he needed help to get around. 'Just extra tired today, so slacking off, as you would say, and riding.'

Cara smiled gently at his attempt at humour.

'What's your name?' the little boy asked, looking up at Cara from his father's knee.

'My name is Cara-Rose. What's yours?' Cara asked, even though Jeremy had told her his name. She saw David flinch at the use of her full name.

'Brandon David Hayle.'

'That is a very nice name.'

The little boy tucked his head into his father's collar.

'Brandon.'

'Nannie,' the little boy squealed. He jumped from David's knee and ran to the back door where a woman in her fifties, dressed in black, stood. Her grey-streaked hair sat bundled on top of her head, and her brown eyes studied Cara.

'Come and see Grandad and Great Nan.'

The woman took the child's hand and looked into David's eyes before turning into the house.

'I should go,' Cara said. She wasn't part of this family and never could be.

'No,' David said. He reached up and grabbed her hand.

'Yes.'

'I'll call you a taxi.' He choked over the quiet words.

'No, I'll walk.' Cara pulled her hand away. *I shouldn't have come.*

'Let me come with you?' Jeremy asked. 'Fancy giving me a push.'

'That would be nice,' Cara said.

David

David stared out over the back lawn; he turned as his grandfather came out the wire door. His dark hair was now grey, and his eyes squinted in the winter sun. He stood tall, with years of Navy service embedded in him. He kept his back straight with the help of a stick.

'Come sit with me,' he said as he sat on one of the wicker chairs beside the coffee table.

David pushed himself up and joined his grandfather.

'How's Grandma?' he asked.

'Brandon's giving her something to smile about.'

David knew bits of the family history. He knew this was the house his grandmother had grown up in, that Frank Kelly had lived in the house next door and had been his grandmother's friend from childhood, and that her first husband was his brother. He knew his grandparents had met in Fremantle during the Second World War. David's mother had been six when his grandparents met, she'd only ever known Grandad as her father.

'You don't have to stay in an unhappy marriage nowadays, David,' his grandfather said.

'I do, Grandad, if I want to see Brandon.' Alice had threatened him and told him she would, and could, stop him from taking Brandon out of the country for a family vacation that was being planned. When Frank Kelly passed away, the vacation was brought forward, and Alice did not make it hard for him to take Brandon away this time.

'I'm sorry,' his grandfather said. 'Sometimes you have to hold onto what you can.' He patted David's hand. 'Come inside and see your grandmother.'

Chapter Nineteen

Cara

The winter sun warmed Cara's face as she walked beside Jeremy. He was fit and strong and didn't need her to push his chair. There was hope he would soon no longer need the wheelchair, but sometimes, the steps forward stalled, and today was one of those days. They strolled past the primary school and around the hospital, the green trees blowing in the gentle breeze.

'Are you hungry?' Jeremy asked.

Surprisingly, Cara was. 'Yes, *The Norfolk*'s not far, let's see if we can get something to eat.'

Cara stood staring at the two stone steps at the front door of the *Norfolk Hotel*. They might have been two hundred as far as she was concerned; there was no way Jeremy would be able to make it into the hotel.

'I'm good,' Jeremy said. He pushed himself to stand, Cara took his arm, and he leaned on the wheelchair.

'Hey mate, you don't need to do that,' a voice called from inside, followed by a face at the doorway. 'We have a ramp around the corner. I'll show you.'

The ramp around the corner was easy to access, and soon, Cara and Jeremy were seated at a table in a quiet corner of the alfresco dining area. Plants hung in baskets, and the cool wind was kept away by the solid stone walls.

'Sorry about that, I need to get a sign for that door,' the same face said.

'Yes, you do,' Cara answered.

'Don't make a fuss, Cara,' Jeremy said.

'No, mate, she's right, I should. What can I get you?'

Cara ordered wine, Jeremy a beer, and the menu was brought. When Jeremy tried to pay for the drinks, his money was refused.

'How are you really?' Cara asked.

'Really ... some days are better than others ... but I am doing okay. The plane trip was difficult, very long.'

He hesitated, then asked, 'Have you heard any more from Marion?'

'Only that she is coming over in September for the court case.'

'My little girl?' Jeremy smiled at this question.

'She is doing great.' Cara beamed. Then she said, 'Jeremy, I don't understand Marion.'

'If I wasn't so useless ...' Jeremy slammed his fists into his legs. 'I could ....'

'Hey, you're not useless.' Cara grabbed his hands.

'I'm not putting Jennifer through a blood test to prove anything, it's cruel.'

'She is your daughter, Sharon said. The courts must rule in your favour.'

'Not if I can't look after her.'

'They can't discriminate because of the wheelchair – they can't.'

'I can't even get a visa to stay longer. I have to leave when the court case is over.' His frustration surface.

'It's not your fault.' Cara squeezed his fingers.

'I'm on my own. They will hold that against me.'

'Sharon left Jennifer with me, not her mother. She didn't tell her mother about her, and I promised Sharon I would look after her. If she wanted her mother to have custody, she would have told her about Jennifer. She would have said so.' Although Cara knew Sharon had expected to return to Jennifer when she recovered.

'She's her grandmother.'

'You are her father.'

'I can't disrupt Jennifer's life all the time. She doesn't even know who I am. She doesn't know Marion.' He pleaded with Cara. 'You are the only one she knows.'

'She'll get to know you; she will love you.' Cara pushed an unruly strand of hair from his eyes. 'We can't let Marion take her away. Why is she doing this? It didn't need to be like this. She could have visited whenever she wanted. Why does she want to take her away?'

Jeremy ran his hands through his light brown hair. It was longer now, curling on the collar of his brown corduroy jacket. He breathed deeply and said, 'It's got to work out.'

Cara wasn't sure who he was trying to convince. She looked into his eyes.

It had been a year since Jeremy found out he had a daughter, a year since that letter arrived, changing their lives.

After that letter arrived, Jeremy insisted on helping Cara with the mortgage. It was the only thing he could do; he could not get a visa to stay in Australia for more than a holiday. Cara did not say no to Jeremy's help. She would have lost her apartment without it.

'I will keep Sharon's memory alive for Jennifer,' Cara said. 'She is little, and her mother will be a memory for her, a beautiful picture on the shelf with lots of stories about her as she grows older.' *A memory with pictures and kind words.*

'But she needs to know who you are, that you are her father, not just a visitor who comes and goes in her life. I hoped Marion would be part of that. Not all this.'

Chapter Twenty

Cara

The next day, Saturday, Cara worked at Myer in the city. Her heart jumped when she saw David waiting at the staff entrance, and she left the building.

'Can we talk?'

Cara nodded.

'Can you come to dinner?'

Cara looked at her work clothing, a black skirt, white shirt, black jacket, and flat shoes. 'I'm not dressed ....'

'You are perfect.'

Cara felt her cheeks warm at his words, and she saw how nervous he was. 'I need to call Liz.'

The streets of Perth were crowded with workers rushing to get home and Saturday night revellers looking to get an early start to their evening. Cara and David found a phone box in Piccadilly Arcade. Then they wandered down the arcade into the Hay Street Mall, and down London Court, with its imitation Tudor buildings and clock tower with its knights jousting every hour on the hour.

The lights in the buildings went out, leaving only shop window displays to fill the darkness. Dirt and leaves flicked up and raced down St Georges Terrace as the traffic hurried by. Cara shivered. David put his arm around her shoulder, and she stared into his eyes.

'It's going to rain, we should hurry.' He took his coat off and wrapped it around her. Rain began to fall as they ran into the shelter of the foyer of the Parmelia Hilton on Mill Street.

David

At a table in front of a log fire, in the Adelphi restaurant, David and Cara ordered food and drink. Low lighting created an elegant ambience, and the tables were set with candles and silverware.

David ran his fingers around his collar and loosened his tie. He wasn't ten years old and sitting in the principal's office, so why did he feel like it?

Cara fidgeted with her fingers; her curls looked wind-swept and damp. He wanted to run his hands through them but...

Until the funeral, he'd had no contact with Cara since he'd last seen her in Austria, she hadn't replied to his letter. But he knew she'd read his letter telling her he was getting married. He knew pieces of her life that involved Jeremy, and he grieved with her at the loss of Sharon.

'How have you been?' he asked. Cara looked at him, a querying smile on her face.

What is wrong with me?

'I am well, how are you?'

'I'm sorry that was stupid. I want to talk to you. I want you to know,' he said.

What could he tell her? The truth. He missed her. He loved her.

'David.' Cara whispered his name.

'I told Alice I was leaving her,' he blurted out.

A waiter came to the table with the bottle of wine David had ordered, and the conversation ceased. The wine poured, he sampled it and nodded his approval, and the waiter filled the glasses. All the while, Cara kept her eyes on him.

When they were alone, he said, 'Alice wasn't pregnant when we got married.' Those words hurt more than he thought possible. 'We were decorating a nursery, had a home. I thought we were a family.' He took a shuddering breath. 'When Alice told me she'd miscarried, we grieved. I thought she grieved, for our loss, for our child. I thought it brought us closer.' He gulped and swallowed, his eyes smarting. 'Alice was my wife. I had no reason to question her, and then when she was pregnant with Brandon, we attended appointments together.' He stumbled over his words. There was too much Cara shouldn't know.

Cara reached across the table, and he clutched her hands, remembering her touch, the touch of someone he loved. 'I tried to forget you, Cara … be a good husband and father.' Cara's green eyes glistened, a gentle smile encouraged him. 'I have Brandon now.'

'Yes,' she whispered. The empathy in her eyes, her joy at that. He needed to tell her what he could of the truth. 'I found out Alice lied last Christmas, and I told her I was leaving.' Forcing words out. 'She will take Brandon away from me if I try, cut me out of his life.'

Cara's grip on his hand tightened. He saw her bite back her tears. He couldn't tell Cara how Alice would do that. How she would scheme and drag Cara into it. Sometimes, he wondered why he'd been so gullible and easy to control.

'You can't let her keep you away from Brandon,' Cara implored. 'No matter what. You have to stay with him. Don't lose your little boy, not for anything.' He understood what she was telling him.

'I won't lose Brandon. I won't let Alice take Brandon from me. But it's the lie – she did it so easily.'

Cara shook her head. 'Brandon's all that matters.'

'Yes, but what happens when he gets older and sees the lies? How will I explain to him?'

Cara pulled a hand from his and ran her fingers across her cheeks. 'You must be in his life. He must have a family.' Her words sliced deep into his heart; he could see how much this mattered to her. He knew her parents had died in a car accident when she was a baby, and he remembered holding her in his arms in Austria as she struggled with a nightmare. What had happened to Cara?

He kissed the hand he held. He'd never forgotten her; he knew he never would.

The waiter coughed discreetly as he brought their meal; he placed the dishes on the table, and then they were alone. When Cara took her wine glass in her hand, the contents sploshed around the sides. 'Let's eat,' she said.

The food was highly regarded and talked about, but it might have been bread and water as far as David was concerned.

He watched Cara push the portion she had put on her plate around, hardly touching a bite, but she drank the wine and the coffee and cake they ordered.

Too soon, it was time to go, and he walked her out to the Taxi rank, desperate to hold her, to pull her into his arms and never let her go. He opened the taxi door for her, and she stood before him, curls blowing in the wind. Pushing them back, he took her face in his hands and lowered his forehead to hers. When Cara pulled away, he said, 'May I see you again?'

'I would like that.' She turned and sat in the taxi.

He watched it drive away as rain spattered his face.

Chapter Twenty-one

Cara

Cara answered a knock on the door.

'I was hoping you would be home.' The speaker wore a dark purple suit with white buttons down the front and on the sleeve cuffs. Cara recognised it as Chanel. 'I'm Jessica Hayle, David's mother. May I speak to you?'

Cara remembered Jessica from Father Kelly's funeral.

'Please come in.' Cara shook the hand offered and stepped aside to allow Jessica into the apartment, showing her onto the balcony before she prepared tea. Cara placed the pot and cups on the white wicker table and sat on one of the plastic chairs in the warm afternoon sun.

'I'm sorry to disturb you,' Jessica said.

'I hope tea is alright?' Cara thought she kept her voice even. What she wanted to say was, why are you here, what do you want?

'Tea is fine. I am pleased to meet you. David told me about you.'

Really?

Jessica stirred her tea and looked out over the balcony as if she was trying to decide what to say. She sipped her tea before speaking. 'I was sorry that you thought we would make David choose between us and you.'

'I couldn't ask him to do that. I couldn't …,' Cara murmured.

'I understand.' Jessica put her cup on the table. 'David would have kept his word to you, no matter the cost. He knew the implication of his decision about Alice. She is the daughter of a major business partner, and a merger was being planned.'

Cara looked over the balcony. She remembered David's promise. She thought she had done the right thing. It had to be for something. *It was, for something, a little boy called Brandon.*

Jessica said, 'David's father is the son of a business associate of my father and my American grandmother; we grew up together. He is a kind and gentle person, and he looked after me and my brother when we were young. It was easy to say yes when he asked me to marry him. David was also the big brother who looked after the girls as they grew, and Alice was one of those girls. When they announced their intention to get engaged, we were happy; he seemed happy. But then he met you.'

Cara didn't know what to say.

'David's father wanted to meet you,' Jessica said.

'To see if I was good enough,' Cara said out loud, unthinking.

'No, no.'

'I'm sorry I didn't mean ….'

'Don't think so badly of us. David would not be the man he is today without his father's influence.'

Tears threatened to spill over Cara's warm cheeks, she pushed them back with her fingers.

'Mimi,' a little voice called from inside the apartment.

'I'm here,' Cara said. Pushing her chair back, she stood, opened the sliding door and picked up a little girl who was wandering around the living room rubbing her eyes. Cara carried her out onto the balcony, and she sat with her on her knee. 'Did you have a nice sleep?'

'Mmm.'

The little girl curled in her lap had honey-brown skin, dark blonde curls, blue eyes, and a look of David about her, but only because David and Jeremy looked so much alike.

'This is Jennifer,' Cara said.

Jessica reached out and stroked the little girl's cheek. 'She could be Brandon's sister; they look alike.'

'She is not.'

'Yes, I know. She looks like her father.'

'She does.'

Cara didn't know how much a parent and child would share as they got older, she had never had that experience, but it seemed as if David had told Jessica many things. The sun moved west, shading the veranda, a chilling breeze blew in over the river and the tea in the pot cooled.

Cara shivered. 'Come inside, it's getting cold.'

Inside, Cara turned the gas heater up and put the electric kettle on; she remade the tea and filled the empty cups. The little girl sat on a rug in front of the fire and played while Cara and Jessica sat at the green and white laminate table with matching chairs.

'I suppose you wonder why I'm here?' Jessica said.

Yes.

'I'm sorry, I'm not sure ... I wanted to meet you,' Jessica hesitated. 'David didn't understand why you went back to Australia without him. He kept his word to his sisters, but as soon as they were back in London, he booked a ticket; even though he didn't know where you lived, he knew he would find you. He hoped we could forgive him for any problems he might cause. We only ever wanted him to be happy.'

Cara stared dumbly at the tea in her cup.

Jessica glanced at the little girl by the fire. 'I was sorry to hear about your friend.'

'Thank you.'

'Alice's announcement changed everything for David. I didn't think she would go as far as she did; he grieved for that child. He struggles with that truth; he tries to keep his family together... he thinks we don't see,' Jessica said.

'He has Brandon now,' Cara whispered.

'Yes, he loves Brandon.'

'Brandon must have a family,' Cara said. *He must have a family.*

'Alice is a good mother to Brandon,' Jessica said.

'And David is a good father.'

'He is.'

'That is all that matters,' Cara whispered the words. *A family to love him.*

'Yes.'

Cara's tears overflowed, and Jessica reached out and wiped them away. 'I'm sorry, perhaps you shouldn't know all this.'

Cara knew some of this. David had told her some of this. Cara took Jessica's hand. 'David loves Brandon,' was all she could say.

Chapter Twenty-two

Cara

The next day, Cara sat on a bench under a gum tree and watched children playing. She wrapped her green scarf around her neck and buttoned up her Country Road green and brown herringbone coat, bought at last year's winter sale for 50% off – the 50% off and her staff discount made it affordable. Size 10, she thought might be too tight, but it fitted perfectly. She wondered why the children had discarded their coats as the icy wind chopping up the water along the river chilled her.

'They never seem to mind the cold,' Jeremy said from beside her.

'No.'

'He's happier today,' Jeremy nodded towards David, who was sitting building castles in the sand with the two children.

Cara turned to face him and saw for the first time what she should have seen all along.

'You love David?'

'Of course, I love David; he's done so much for me.' Jeremy's tone was a little too tight, a little too abrupt.

'Jeremy!'

'He doesn't know.'

'Are you sure?'

Jeremy looked into her eyes and said, 'He loves you, Cara.'

'What can I do?' Cara asked.

'Hold on to what you can.'

'Oh, Jeremy.' Cara clutched his hand.

'Hey, you two,' David called. He dusted the dirt from his jeans and zipped his leather bomber jacket as he came out of the sandpit. His brown curls were gelled back. He smiled gently at Cara, and her heart crumbled. When his eyes connected with hers, she remembered the first time he'd done that, the first time she'd remembered the wild lilies of her childhood. 'They seem to like each other.' He stretched his back as he looked at the children.

The outing had been arranged when Jessica visited. The river foreshore, a grassy park with a children's playground, across the road from Cara's apartment. A chance for the children to meet and play, a chance for Cara to spend time with David.

It was also time for Jeremy to share with Jennifer. He'd seen her twice since he'd met her – in October last year, for her second birthday, and early in the New Year when he visited with his mother and sister so they could meet Jennifer.

Every visit was a first visit to Jennifer; she was too young to remember the earlier ones, and this visit was no different.

David sat on the bench beside her. Cara ached, she wanted to put her arms around him, pull his face to hers, and caress his lips. She wanted to let him know she was there. She could feel his body beside her, the tension, the longing. He knew she was there.

'Daddy,' the little boy said as he stood in front of David. David brushed sand from the blue and yellow Golden State Warriors jacket with the number 5 on the front that Brandon held. He pulled it around him and zipped it up before Brandon clambered onto his knee.

Cara lifted Jennifer onto her knee, zipped her pink jacket up and brushed sand from her denim overalls. Jennifer tucked her head into Cara's shoulder, away from the unfamiliar men she shared the bench with.

'Shall we get ice cream?' Cara asked.

'It's winter,' David said.

'It's Australia,' Cara replied. 'There's never a time you don't get ice cream. There is a shop up near the ferry jetty.'

David lifted Brandon onto his shoulders, and Cara could see how much Jeremy wanted to be able to do this as well. He was walking today, only needing an elbow crutch for support if he got tired. She said to Jennifer, 'Hold hands and swing with us.' The little girl looked unsure, but she took Cara's hand, and the hand Jeremy offered her.

'Not too high,' Cara said.

As they wandered along the river foreshore, Cara thought, *a happy family to anyone passing by.*

David

'Where's Mummy?' Brandon asked as he sat on David's shoulders. David tugged him down and pulled him close to his chest. 'She's at home.'

'Why?'

'Mummy couldn't come with us this time, she has work to do. We will see her soon when we get home, is that okay?'

'Yes.'

Brandon wiggled out of David's arms and scampered across the grass to look at the water, Jennifer ran to join him.

'Stay away from the edge,' Cara said, wasting her breath as the two children knelt on the embankment staring down at the brackish water swirling by.

David looked into Cara's eyes. She'd heard every word Brandon said, he could see that, and he knew Cara would never come between Brandon and his mother.

Hold on to what you can, Grandad had said.

He had two weeks.

Jeremy sat on the bench beside the river and said, 'I'll watch them. Go get the ice cream.'

Cara's curls swirled around her face as he walked beside her. He reached out and pushed the strands away, caressing her cheek. She stopped and stared into his eyes before turning and continuing to walk. As they walked together, her hand brushed the back of his before her fingers wound around his, and their hands bound together.

Hold onto what you can.

Chapter Twenty-three

David

The drive down south through the forests and the country towns to the Caves House in Yallingup took longer than expected. Cara's old 1970 Holden Gemini kept overheating, and there were stops along the way to top up the radiator with water she carried.

The smell of hot radiator water mingled with the scent of eucalyptus leaves. Magpies warbled in the gently moving trees as David and Cara sat at a wooden bench in an off-road parking bay, drinking lukewarm coffee from a flask.

David pulled his jacket tight. 'Are you cold?'

Cara nodded and he fetched the blanket from the boot of the car and wrapped it around her. Cara held the blanket together as The Eagles sang *Hotel California* on the car radio while they waited for the radiator to cool.

Tyres scrunched on the gravel road, as they pulled into the Caves Hotel's car park, the hissing radiator bellowing steam. David pulled the parking brake on and turned the engine off.

I'll have to do something about that.

He'd asked Cara to come away with him yesterday. She'd hesitated, but then she looked into his eyes, placed her arms around his neck, and whispered, 'Yes.'

As he stood on the top of the stone steps, cases in hand, David understood why Cara had suggested coming here. A cold wind blew across the manicured lawns and bent branches on trees covered in green leaves. He saw joy in Cara's eyes as she looked around and heard her breathe the salty air.

Cara stared out the window of a room decorated in pastel colours with pink and purple floral curtains and a matching doona on the queen bed that stood on wooden floors. David put his arms around her and turned her to face him. 'Only if you want to, we can just spend time together, if that is all you want.'

'Let's go for a walk.' She took his hand, and they left the room, bags still on the floor.

The pathway to the ocean was marked Ghost Trail, and Cara told him the story of the young girl who died on her wedding night and whose ghost now wanders the grounds. He was too practical to believe that, but he held Cara's hand tight as they wandered along the dirt trail under overhanging trees that moaned in the wind. The trail opened onto a bitumen road leading to a grassed embankment overlooking the ocean.

Huge waves rolled across the water, thudding onto the shore, washing away the sand and filling the air with salt. It was difficult to breathe the freezing air, the blue sky and pale sunshine offered no warmth. He pulled his scarf around his neck and held Cara close. She seemed to gain strength from the sea and salt, standing straight and breathing in the frigid air, her face tight from the chill. She turned to him and said, 'I tried to forget you, David.'

***

Upstairs later, they stood together, unsure. He lowered his head and put his lips to hers. They were cold, but as she explored his mouth, they warmed. Cara pushed his jumper over his head. She fumbled with the buttons on his shirt before helping him with his jeans.

He was anxious, like he was making love for the first time, as he stood in his shorts before her, and could not hide this feeling. Cara trembled as he removed her clothing. She stood before him in her camisole and nickers, and he ran his fingers through her hair, kissing her mouth, face, and neck.

Then he was in bed with her, making love with her, gently and desperately, needing the contact only making love could give him. He gave her his body and his soul, all of him, until there was nothing left to give. He folded Cara into his arms as she slept, wanting to hold her forever.

Cara stirred in his arms, and he ran his fingers through her curls. Three days. He had three days to spend with her. Brandon had gone off to the country town of York with David's mother and grandparents to visit family on a farming property. Jennifer was staying with Liz and Mike to spend time with Jeremy, who was going to have to go to court and prove he was capable of being a father to her. Brandon was his son. He was his father, but he knew that Alice could dictate the future of his relationship with his son.

He stared at the roof and tightened his arm around Cara. The guilt he felt was for Cara and what he was doing to her. He tried to keep his home together and make a family for Brandon. But it was harder and harder to do that since he found out Alice had lied to him. Their life together, from the outside, appeared happy, but that was the veneer they showed the world. There was no love in that life, and he wondered how long he could keep pretending before Brandon noticed.

He wanted to leave Alice and make a life with Cara, a life that would include Brandon. But he knew Alice would fight him if he tried, and he knew she could take Brandon. She'd already shown him how she would do that. He closed his eyes and pushed thoughts of Alice away. He was with Cara. Alice could wait.

Cara

Cara curled into David's body, and he tightened his arm around her; he loved her, but he could never be hers. She listened to his heartbeat and his breathing as he slept peacefully. Moving gently away from him, she swung her legs over the side of the bed, ran her hands through her curls then picked her camisole and nickers from the floor and pulled them on before tiptoeing across the room to look out the window.

The grassed gardens shone in the coming sunset. Evening sunshine turned the leaves red and gold, and Cara could see the outline of the ocean through the treetops. She jumped when David put his arms around her and kissed the scar on her shoulder. She turned to face him, and he said, 'Will you tell me?' She took a deep breath and nodded.

David tugged the doona from the bed and wrapped it around them as they sat on the settee under the window. Cara pushed at her fingernail, her head bowed staring at the floor, fear and uncertainty surrounding her.

'It's okay, you can tell me.' David tipped her chin, so she was looking into his eyes. 'Whatever you want. If you're ready.'

If I'm ready.

Cara trusted David completely. He held her hand gently, securely. She would tell him everything, everything she had never told anyone else.

November 1988

Cold air blew around Cara as she stood before the faded white building, its windows dark and looming. She raised her hand to knock on the old wooden door and imagined living there, imagined being forced to work there until the day she died. How many women had lived in this building, run by Catholic Nuns, known as a Magdalen Laundry? Her mother was one. Fallen women locked up for their protection, for the protection of society. She heard plaintive cries on the wind, echoing down the years, and Cara saw gaunt and terrified faces staring at the windows. She tilted her head to see the cross on top of the building. The world around her spun, the building seemed to fall towards her, and she raised her hands, holding it back.

'You alright, Miss?' the taxi driver called.

'I'm okay,' Cara said. She turned to the driver and said, 'You will wait, won't you?'

'I'll wait.' He was an older man, with grey hair and a portly belly, somehow reassuring to Cara.

Cara steadied herself and knocked on the door. An elderly lady, seemingly dressed in rags, opened it. As Cara's eyes adjusted to the dim lighting, she realised she wore an old-fashioned Nun's habit, like the sisters at her school had worn.

'Can I help you?'

'I'm looking ....' Cara didn't know what to say. It was so many years ago. Would anyone remember? Would they care? 'My mother.'

The old nun looked at Cara. 'Why would your mother be here?'

'She was sent here. A long time ago.'

'There are only a few of us here now. Come, I will show you.'

Cara stepped inside the building. Damp and cold hit her. Dark wooden floors creaked under her feet, and religious pictures hung on the gloomy walls. She trailed down the hallway, listening to the old nun rambling until she stopped in front of her, turned, and asked, 'What is her name?'

'My name is Cara-Rose Maloney. I think my mother's name is Margaret.'

'Margaret, Margaret ... I can show you where Margaret is.'

Cara shivered, not from the cold. They continued down the hallway until the nun stopped at a doorway and pushed it open. 'Here, she is ... here...'

Cara saw sunlight through the open door, and as her eyes became accustomed to the light, she saw rows and rows of headstones neatly lining *the green lawn.*

'Who are you?' a voice asked from inside the building. 'What are you doing here?'

'She is looking for Margaret....'

'Come now, Sister, go back to your room. You know we don't let strangers in.'

'She's looking for her mother ....'

'I will help her; you go back to your room.'

Cara watched as the old nun shuffled back inside past the speaker, who placed a hand gently on her shoulders and repeated, 'Go back to your room.'

Cara turned to look at the graveyard.

'Why have you come here?' she was asked.

'My mother,' Cara said. She turned to the speaker, a younger woman in a knee-length navy blue dress with a white collar. She wore a navy veil with a white band on her head, exposing her hair at the front.

'I have an appointment.'

'Here?'

'No, at Our Lady of Mercy House.' Cara stepped onto the lawn, overwhelmed by the number of headstones spreading out in front of her, each with many names etched on it. She stumbled across the lawn and rested her hand on one of the stones.

'So many.'

'It was a long time ago. You should come back inside.'

'Not so long for some,' Cara said. The date she was looking at read 1983.

'Yes. Come back inside.' Cara was escorted back into the building, a gentle but firm hand on her back guiding her to the front door.

'For some, it is better left alone. I hope you find what you're looking for.'

For a moment, Cara had hope. She hurried back to the waiting taxi. The driver opened the door, his brown eyes querying.

'Let's go,' Cara said as she sat in the back seat of the grey vehicle.

The streets of Dublin were full of celebrations for the city's thousand-year-old birthday, something Cara had not been aware of when she'd made her bookings. Still, she had to find answers, and Dublin was where they were.

Cara sat in an office on one side of a dark timber table. The woman opposite her was dressed in a business suit and had short dark hair. The only suggestion of any religious order was a cross on a chain around her neck. She shouldn't have been surprised. The building seemed so unreligious—a square grey brick structure with a flat roof—not what she thought a church in an ancient city would look like.

'I have read your letter,' the woman said. 'What do you hope to find out here?'

What do I want to know?

'I think my ….' Cara had it all planned, all worked out, what she would say … why was it so hard?

'In my letter, I told you I believe my mother was sent to the laundry in High Park.'

'There were many women at that facility.'

Facility.

'I thought her situation might have been unique.'

And there was that look in the eyes of the woman sitting across from her, the look Cara had seen so many times over her life. She knew she would get no answers here, but she had to try.

'My mother?'

'Committed the worst possible sin, one that can never be forgiven. I am surprised you would even want to know who she was.'

'She was my mother.'

'Then you are lucky she was sent away from you to save your soul.'

Cara sat dumbfounded, she hadn't expected to be treated with any care or kindness, but she hadn't expected this either.

118

'She was young.'

'She was a whore.'

Cara clasped her hands together. 'Can you tell me if she is still alive?'

'I cannot.'

'Why?'

'There are many women with similar names.'

'How many women were in her situation? Surely you could find her.'

Cara knew she was going nowhere. She knew she was getting no answers here.

'Please, I've come such a long way.'

'Then you should have stayed away.'

'Where is your kindness, your compassion? You spout all this religious garbage, and your hearts are black ....'

'You had better leave.'

Cara pushed her chair back and rested her hand on the desk. She wouldn't get any answers, but she wasn't finished. 'Jesus forgave Mary Magdalene. You named your institutes after her, but you have no forgiveness in your souls. What would he say?'

For a minute, Cara saw the woman's eyes soften, but years of doctrine could not melt in seconds.

Cara turned and walked away, out of the office, out of the unreligious building. She was shaking when she reached the waiting taxi, her stomach turning, and she struggled to walk. She leaned against the car to breathe and took the bottle of water the driver offered her.

***

1992

Cara said, 'I told you my parents died in a car accident. I think my father did, but I never knew my mother. I wasn't brought up by a family. I lived in a … it's not called an orphanage anymore, now it's a home for girls, less of a stigma for those running it, I suppose. I thought everyone lived like I did. After I started going to school, I began to realise my life was different from my classmates. It was even different from the other girls at the home.' She sucked in a deep breath. 'Sharon came to the home when I was about four. She was funny and naughty, and sometimes we got into trouble. Sharon was a faster runner than me. I learned early not to tell.' Cara's voice faded to a whisper with that memory.

'I'm so sorry.' David ran his fingers through her hair.

'My poor, silly girl,' Cara mumbled. Her gaze wandered around the room. David pulled the blanket tighter.

'Sharon's mother planned to migrate to Perth, and she came and took Sharon home with her when we were seven. Most of the girls went to live with families, but I stayed in the girl's home. I thought I must have been very wicked that my mother didn't come and get me, that no one wanted me. That was reinforced by some of the Sisters around me. One day I was setting the table for dinner, it was cold, and I dropped a plate. Why was she so cruel to a child … I tried to defend myself, but … I was little. I …'

Cara reached around to her shoulder and ran her hand across the scar. David ran his fingers across his cheeks before pulling her hands together and kissing her fingers.

'I was stitched up, given some sleeping medicine, and put to bed. I didn't know this wasn't normal. It was all I knew. I heard lots of awful words, words like *she's no better than her mother, she will only get into trouble, and why are we wasting our time with her?* I didn't know what they meant.'

David's arms tightened around her. She was safe with him. He pushed her tangled hair away and wiped tears from her face.

'You don't have to say anymore,' he said.

'I want you to know.' *I need you to know. To love me enough to forgive me.*

'Mother Superior died when I was fourteen, but before that, I was made to listen. I had to sit by her bed in the semi-dark room.' Cara shuddered at that memory of the dark and cold room, the smell of incense and burning candles. The frail, withered woman lying in the bed. The woman who held onto her hatred until the day she died.

She pulled back her memories and said, 'Mother Superior told me my mother had committed the worst possible sin. She'd led a good man to damnation, and she'd been sent back to Ireland in disgrace. She told me it had been decided that I would stay in the convent and atone for her sins because no one could or would ever love me.'

Now out of words, Cara stared at the floor. She was older now and understood the power of indoctrination, but she could not understand the cruelty it excused.

'I ran away that night. It was the middle of winter, and I didn't have much money. I didn't know what I was doing or where I was going. I ended up under the railway bridge in Fremantle. There were other people under there, and it was warm by the fire. They shared their food, but I didn't understand there would be a cost. I thought I killed him, but he was only wet with a bruised head when the police fished him out of the river. That's when I met Father Kelly.'

Cara smiled at the memory of that cold, freezing morning, of a warm cup of Milo, a piece of cake, and a kind and gentle man who kept his word to her.

'He was kind to me. I stayed with him and his housekeeper until he found me a home with Liz and her family. I didn't know how wrong my life had been until then.' Cara shivered in the cooling room and David pulled the blanket tighter around them.

'Father Kelly told me what he knew about my mother when I was older. She was a Novice Sister; he told me she loved my father, but she never told anyone who he was. She was the one who took all the blame and all the shame. The Sisters must have known; there were whispers about a young priest who died in an accident before I was born. No one ever thought I was listening. His car ran off a bridge. They said it was an accident, it had to be an accident for him to be buried properly.'

Cara swallowed her tears. 'Father Kelly told me my mother had been sent to a place called High Park in Ireland, *a place for fallen women*. I was left in the orphanage. I tried to get answers in Dublin, but there were none. No one would say anything.'

Cara had kept this secret locked in her heart for so long. No one knew the truth, and she sometimes wondered what of the truth she knew. She had never spoken about her parents to anyone except the lie that they died when she was a baby.

She had lied her way through her life, every little lie adding to the bigger one. The trip to Ireland to visit her grandparents before meeting the girls in London was a lie. All her efforts to find out about her mother had been a waste.

'Maybe Mother Superior was right. Maybe I don't deserve to be loved,' Cara mumbled.

'She was not right,' David spoke firmly. He turned Cara's face to his. 'She was not right. I love you.'

'I've made a mess of your life.' Cara sucked in a breath, ran her fingers under her eyes.

'You have not.'

'Can you forgive me?' *Can you love me enough?*

'For what?' Concern shrouded David's face.

'For what my mother did.'

'Your mother did nothing wrong; she fell in love and was never given the chance to know you. She would have loved you.' Concern turned to compassion.

Like a child, Cara asked, 'Do you think so?'

'Yes, Cara-Rose, I'm sure she would love you, as I love you.'

Cara swallowed. 'I imagine my mother loved me. I push the other stuff away and lock it in the cupboard in my head, but sometimes it escapes. All the words rush at me, telling me I am unworthy of being loved. I can't lie anymore. I'm … I'm tired.'

David kissed her fingers, then cupped her face, drawing her close. He caressed her lips before saying, 'You never have to lie again. I love you; I will always love you. Don't think you are unworthy of being loved. I love you, and I understand.'

'You can't let Alice take Brandon from you,' Cara said. 'He must have a father and a mother to love him, a family; you have to stay for him.'

David tilted her head so she was looking into his eyes and said, 'I promise you, I will always look after Brandon. And I promise you, no matter how long it takes, we will be together.'

Cara rested her head on his chest and listened to his heartbeat. 'No matter how long,' she whispered.

David

David held Cara curled in his arms. He pulled the blanket tighter around her and held her until her breathing became steady, and he realised she had fallen asleep. He pushed her hair from her face and whispered, 'While I breathe, you will be loved. I will be with you, even when we are apart.'

He carried her to the bed, lay her down, and tucked the blankets around her before sitting back on the chair and staring out the window. The sky went dark, and stars popped into sight.

David woke early the following day and moved Cara gently off his arm, but she stirred. 'Go back to sleep, it's early.' He pulled the blankets around her shoulder. *What are we going to do?* There was no answer to that question.

He pulled on his tracksuit and running shoes and locked the door behind him. He loved to run. It kept him fit and gave him time to think. There was nothing he could offer Cara. He wouldn't ask her to be with him, to be his *Mistress*, such an old-fashioned word with terrible implications.

Cara had her life, and he couldn't stay; he had a home with Alice and a life with Brandon.

He ran up the bitumen road and followed it around the cove and down into the bay—the ocean on his left, over the blue scrub bushes boiled with a coming storm. The grey sky was full of threatening black clouds, and the sun peeking over the hilltops barely broke the darkness. As he ran through the Ghost Trail, he could understand the reason for all the stories. Slashes of white stone on the grey cliffs seemed to float over him to his left. Trees shrouded his path, blocking the sunrise, and to his right, a dark ravine threatened if he missed his step.

Rain began to fall, and he ran through the gardens, up the stairs, and into the safety of the hotel lobby. The sky lit up; thunder shattered the silence, and driving rain pelted the roof and windows.

David opened the bedroom door, running shoes in his hand and found Cara staring out the window. She ducked her head as the next bolt of lightning seemed to hit the garden out the window.

'I'm here,' he said, dropping his shoes before wrapping her in his arms.

'Yuk.'

'Yuk!'

'You're all wet.'

Cara giggled and pushed him away before pulling his wet jumper over his head and tossing it on the floor. Water cascaded from the roof, torrents ran down the window, blurring the outside. More thunder rumbled, and lightning flashed. David pulled the curtains shut. For a moment, they stood facing each other. Cara pushed his t-shirt over his head, and he removed the windcheater she wore. Now, she stood before him in her camisole and nickers.

He pushed the camisole over her head, letting it fall to the floor; she stood half-naked in front of him. He bent his head and caressed her breasts with his mouth as Cara ran her hands through his hair, murmuring and gulping for air. He picked her up, and she wrapped her legs around his back as he carried her to the bed. Laying her gently, he pushed his track pants down and reached for the side table.

'Do we have to?' Cara asked.

'I trust you with my life, Cara-Rose. Do you trust me?'

'I do.'

And maybe that was all he could do. That was all they could have. He left the condom in the top drawer and pushed Cara's knickers down.

Cara

Cara woke to the smell of fresh coffee, bacon and toast as David entered the room with a tray. 'Are you hungry?'

'Mmm ....' She stretched her arms above her head, sat and pushed her hair away, letting the blankets fall and wrap around her.

'Food.'

'Food,' Cara replied.

David sat on the bed and put the tray beside her. Cara wrapped her arms around his neck. 'Food,' he said, but it wasn't to happen. He put the tray on the floor, and she pulled his jumper over his head.

Cara kissed David's mouth and his throat; she ran her hands across his chest and down to his belly, pushing his track pants away. He lay back on the bed, and she knelt over him, straddling him, letting him see her, watching him see her. He took her face before running his fingers through her curls. Sitting, he kissed her mouth, her neck, and her breasts before his fingers traced down her stomach to her thighs and between her legs. Cara ran her hands through his hair, caressing the back of his neck until she was gasping for air, and then they lay back on the bed and gave themselves to each other.

The food on the floor was cold when Cara woke, but she was hungry and ate the bacon and toast and washed it down with tepid coffee as she watched David sleep. He opened his eyes.

'Hungry,' Cara said.

He grinned at her, and she said, 'I love you, David.'

'And I you. What …?'

Cara placed her finger on his lips. She had waited for him and wanted to enjoy him, not think about tomorrow; it would come, and when it did, she would think about it.

'Tomorrow is soon enough,' she said.

And he seemed to understand. Tomorrow would come, but not today. Today, they would take the time they could, and they did.

The Caves Hotel is a popular spot for honeymooners, and David and Cara spent the day watching the storm blow itself out as it knocked down trees and dumped water over the garden. Trees dripped icy water on them as they made their way along the Ghost Trail before standing on the top of the steps that led down to the ocean, watching waves roll in to wash away any remaining sand. Eating in front of the fire, they shared their bodies before falling asleep in each other's arms.

Chapter Twenty-four

David

David woke to the sound of feet running in the hallway and voices shouting in the car park. He pulled on his shorts and jumper and opened the door. Two men in scruffy wetsuits with wet, lanky hair stood deep in discussion.

'Anything wrong?' he asked.

'There's been a whale stranding.'

Other doors were opening, and heads peered out to see what the commotion was about.

'Can we help?' David asked.

'Have you got a wetsuit?'

'No.'

The speaker studied David, 'I've got one that will fit. Can you swim?'

Can I swim? Maybe his accent triggered that question. 'Yes.'

'Anyone else.'

By now, the hallway was filling with concerned patrons. 'We are leaving in fifteen minutes if anyone can help.'

David turned back into the room to find Cara pulling on her jeans and jumper. 'I can swim.'

The ride in the back of the ute was cold. Wind howled around them as they huddled on the back tray, with several other helpers. At least yesterday's storms had abated. David stared at the sight before him as the ute turned the headland. On the white sandy beach, bodies lay scattered about, some moving pitifully, some motionless. The rising sun glimmered off grey and blue flesh, flesh that should not be on the sand. The ute screeched into the car park beside other cars, and David helped Cara down, her eyes wide and distressed. She pulled her beanie tight over her red curls.

David was handed an old, crunchy, wet suit. 'When you've changed, can you come down to the water where the boats are?'

'What can I do?' Cara asked.

'We need tea and hot drinks for those already here. Can you help with that?'

'Yes, I can do that.'

Another voice said, 'I need someone to put towels and buckets of water over an animal stuck in the sand. Can you help me?' The question was directed at Cara.

'Tea and hot drinks?'

'Got someone else for that.'

David embraced Cara, kissed her forehead and said, 'I will see you soon.' He watched her walk away beside someone dressed in a high-vis yellow vest and blue overalls.

Cara

Cara walked through desolation, through plaintive cries, squeals, and bodies writhing. That wasn't the worst she saw; the worst was the bodies lying motionless, already beginning to dry even though the sky was grey now and sea spray filled the air. She wiped her cheeks with the back of her fingers.

'Will you be okay on your own?' The speaker surveyed the beach. 'I will try and get someone to come and help you.'

There seemed to be many animals in distress. 'I can manage on my own if need. What do I do?'

'We must keep them wet until we can get them back into the water. There are blankets and towels up the beach and buckets to carry the water. I'll get you some.'

'No, I can do that. You go and help elsewhere.'

Cara raced back up the beach to what she presumed was the operation centre. She grabbed as many blankets as she could carry and ran back to the creature she was helping. Stopping at its head, she whispered, 'You'll be okay. I'm getting you some water.' Then she ran into the cold ocean, forgetting she was clothed, forgetting the strength of the waves until she tripped, but she stayed upright and threw the blankets into the sea. When they were wet through, she dragged them out and placed them over the animal she was attending to. 'I'm going to get some buckets now,' she told it.

Cara ran back up the beach and returned with two buckets. She ran into the water, more carefully this time, filling her buckets. Surprised at how heavy they were, she could only manage one at a time, and left one in the shallows and struggled back to the whale. Cara poured water over the animal, caressing its head as she did, and she saw it turn its eye to look at her. 'I won't let you die,' she said.

She did not know how long she went back and forth to the water filling buckets and keeping her whale wet. Her clothing was soaked; she'd tugged her damp hair under her beanie and thought she should be cold, but she didn't feel cold.

Sometime around the middle of the morning, she was offered a hot coffee and a dry piece of cake, which she scoffed down. She spent the morning talking to and keeping her whale alive. Around the middle of the day, a tarpaulin was dug under the whale to help it remain upright and to allow it to be carried down to the water's edge and towed out to sea.

Cara was humming *Guns and Roses, Patience* when a shadow fell over her, and she looked up into David's exhausted face; she wondered what her face looked like. He wasn't alone – several other helpers were standing around her whale. 'What's the time?' she asked.

'Nearly 3.30 pm.'

David reached out to help her up, and she stumbled into his arms, her legs cramped and unresponsive. He held her tight as she regained strength in her legs.

'You can take your girl up to the fire,' Cara heard.

His girl

Cara looked up into David's eyes and said, 'I'm good – you stay and help.'

'This will be the last one today,' another voice said.

'Are you sure?' David asked Cara.

'Yes.'

Cara held David's hand for support when she knelt to caress her whale. She'd never thought about how a whale's skin would feel, but she could tell they must hurry to get her into the water. Her skin was drying out and no longer felt soft and squishy like a firm tomato. It felt like an old potato, still soft but beginning to crack in places.

'You will be safe now. When you get to the water, swim far out, find your family and don't come back,' she told the animal.

With David's help, Cara stood and moved away as the helpers lifted the whale from the sand. It screeched and cried, writhing and flapping its flutes until it seemed to accept its fate and calmed as those carrying it struggled down to the waiting boat at the water's edge.

Cara wiped her tears away and watched until the boat launched. She turned and forced her unwilling legs to trek up the beach to a fire burning on the sand. A rug was wrapped around her shoulders, and a hot cup of coffee was placed in her hands as she sat near the flames. Then she knew she was cold; her fingers could barely grasp the cup.

David

It was six o'clock and dark when David staggered up the stairs and into the lounge of the Caves House. He was not alone. The

130

conversations that had been faltering on the ride back to the hotel had stopped. He stood in the doorway and saw Cara asleep on a chair before the fire, a blanket tucked around her. She opened her eyes as he stood beside the chair. Cara reached up and took his hand, 'Did she swim away? Is she safe?'

He nodded.

'Hell of a way to spend your honeymoon,' a voice beside him said. And he was about to answer when he realised this was probably all they would have, and he couldn't get any words out.

'No,' Cara said from the chair beside him. 'I wouldn't want it any other way.' Was she talking about the whales?

'Don't rush off tomorrow. Stay as long as you need.'

'Thank you,' Cara replied, pushing herself out of the chair, her damp clothes clinging to her. He could see how tired she was—she could barely walk—and put his arm around her.

'As long as we can have,' he whispered to her.

Upstairs, they showered together before eating the food delivered to the room and collapsing into bed.

Chapter Twenty-five

David

The drive back to the city did not take as long as the drive down south. David had arranged for Cara's radiator to be repaired while they stayed in the hotel. She had objected, but he had insisted.

That night, he slept in her bed with her scent on the linen, and Cara curled into his body after they made love. He soaked the memory in.

Brandon came back from York on Sunday full of tales of his adventures. Cara worked on Monday and picked Jennifer up on Tuesday, telling stories of her adventures. On Wednesday, David visited Cara with Jeremy and Brandon so that *Brandon could play with Jennifer.* Cara worked on Thursday and Saturday, and he had work to do on Friday. Sunday came, and David, Jeremy and Cara took the children to the zoo. A ferry took them across the river' they ate ice cream, and Brandon and Jennifer rode on the merry-go-round. He stood with Cara wrapped in his arms and watched.

His two weeks were over in less than the wink of an eye. The flight back to the USA was booked for Tuesday, August 25th, and there was nothing he could do to change that.

He had one day left, and on that day, Liz and Mike took Jennifer and Jeremy out. Brandon stayed with his grandmother, and David spent the day with Cara. There was so much he wanted to say to her. She knew he loved her, but he told her anyway. She also knew he was leaving her, and there were no words for that.

They sat on the river foreshore, legs over the embankment, boots and shoes beside them, not far from her home. The winter sun was surprisingly warm, and the shade from the green tree was welcome. His coat, suitable for the winter in the US, was too warm for winter in Perth.

'Will you come to the airport tomorrow?' David asked.

Cara nodded.

'I'm sorry.'

Cara looked over the water, 'No, don't say that, I know this is what we must do. I understand.'

'Maybe …'

'No.'

What he wanted and what was going to happen were so far apart. Should he have stayed away and not put Cara through this? He understood now why Cara needed Brandon to have a family; she'd never had one.

He put his arm around her, and she rested her head on his shoulder. He breathed in her scent to remember it always. A little tin dinghy glided by, the occupants waving, and he returned the greeting, it was the only boat on the river. The wake from the dinghy rolled towards them, they would get wet if they didn't move. He helped Cara up, and she wrapped her arms around him and whispered, 'I love you.'

And he loved her. He also loved Brandon, and they would put Brandon's needs first.

Cara

Perth airport was hectic and full of travellers for its location on the corner of a distant continent. David's flight was due to leave at 1:30. Cara stood with Jeremy as David and his family checked in, and all the necessary passports, tickets, and luggage labels were checked and obtained. Jeremy would be staying until the court case in early October.

Jessica took Brandon by the hand and said, 'Let's go and see the planes landing.' The little boy took his grandmother's hand and said, 'Can Jennifer come?'

'Will you come with me?' Jeremy asked, holding out his hand.

His surprise showed when the little girl took his hand and climbed onto his knee. 'Which way to the elevator?' Jeremy asked.

She was alone with David. Cara looked out over the first-floor railing. The escalator carried travellers up and down. People scurried about on the grey and orange carpet, painted columns reached for the ceiling and glass windows flooded the building with light. The beginning of an adventure for some, and for others, time to say goodbye.

In amongst the crowd, David and Cara stood alone. He wrapped her in his arms and whispered, 'I'm sorry.'

'I can wait,' Cara said. And she could; she could wait forever if he could.

'I will wait. We will be together.' He bent his head and touched his forehead to hers.

He kissed her mouth, and she closed her eyes. The salt from his tears mingled with the gentle smile on his lips.

Cara heard the chatter of children before she heard the announcement that their plane was boarding.

Jessica hugged Cara and said, 'I am pleased to have met you.' Then she said to Brandon, 'Say goodbye to Jennifer and Cara.'

The little boy looked shyly at the floor before smiling at Cara and quietly saying, 'Goodbye.' Cara wanted to lift him into her arms, but he wasn't hers. He had a mother who loved him, and that is how it should be.

Cara said, 'Goodbye, Brandon.' Then she said to Jennifer, 'Say goodbye to Brandon.'

The children stood apart before they moved slowly together for a hug. People passing by smiled, oohing and aahing at the children. Cara had her eyes fixed on David and him on her. It was time to go. He picked Brandon up, turned, and walked with Jessica down the mezzanine to the entry, where his grandparents waited.

Cara stood and watched; she didn't move; couldn't move. Jeremy took her hand as the door to the departure lounge swallowed David.

Cara didn't know how long she stood staring at that door. She remembered riding the lift to the observation deck and watching the Qantas jet take off. All the while, The Steve Millar Band song, *Jet Airline*, tumbled around her head: "You know you got to go through hell before you get to heaven."

Chapter Twenty-six

Cara

Cara stood on the corner of Terrace Road and Victoria Street, Perth, a mixture of well-dressed and casually dressed people hurrying around her. She pulled her jacket together and patted her hair down, pushing unruly strands back into the clips holding it in place. She had never been in court before. Todd had insisted that presentation could make or break a case depending on the judge, so there had been a shopping trip for Jeremy.

Cara saw him coming down the hill from the Terrace, walking with the aid of one elbow crutch, his navy-blue pinstriped suit, blue shirt, and dark tie a perfect fit. He'd cut his hair and gelled the curls back away from his eyes. He looked so much like David that Cara caught her breath.

Todd walked beside Jeremy, carrying a briefcase, looking the part of an expensive lawyer, which he was. His designer suit accentuated his slim body, his blond hair short and combed into a wave back from his forehead, his Ray-bans keeping the sun out of his eyes. Todd wasn't Jeremy's lawyer – he was David's – and he couldn't practice in Australia – was there only for moral support.

Cara understood now. She knew David employed Jeremy and had done so since the accident. It ensured he had a good wage, enabled him to pay for his trips back and forth to Australia, and provided him with the legal and medical help he needed.

The court conference was set for 9:30 on Wednesday, 14th October 1992, one day before Jennifer's third birthday. Jeremy's lawyer, Johnathon Gordon, waited at the entrance to the conference room. Squinting in the morning sunshine that poured through the massive window, she pulled Jeremy into her embrace before taking his hand, his nerves running through her body. She pushed the lock of his hair that fell across his forehead away and said, 'We can do this.'

He nodded.

**

The courthouse was busy, the hallways and foyer dotted with groups of people chatting and revisiting through paperwork, but the courtroom they entered on the third floor was quiet and private. Marion and her husband sat on one side of the wooden table facing Jeremy and his lawyer on the opposite side. Cara and Todd sat further down the table. There were two other people in the court. One was the lawyer appointed by the courts to represent Jennifer's best interests. She had not seen the other person before.

The initial hearing in September had failed to resolve the issues. Marion insisted that Jennifer must be hers to bring up as Jeremy was a single man living alone, and would not know how to bring up a child, so now they were in conference to decide what was in Jennifer's best interest.

The Court Registrar sat at the head of the table, Jennifer's legal counsel closest to her on the long side of the table, the Family Consultant next to her. Cara's heart sank – Todd had said that a female judicial officer, especially one closer to Marion's age, might make it more difficult for Jeremy to plead his case. They were all about Marion's age, or slightly younger.

'While we look at this matter in regard to what is in the child's best interest,' the Registrar said, 'the discussion will remain open, provided it remains amicable.'

Marion leapt in straight away, outlining the events that had led up to this moment, and then summarized, 'I can provide Jennifer with a proper family, a home with a garden to play in, and I've already enrolled her in school.' She'd talked for the past fifteen minutes, telling the Registrar and Jennifer's lawyer about the wonderful life Jennifer would have when she took her back to London. While it was obvious she would not live with her father, she'd said, he would always be welcome in her life if he wanted to be. Jennifer would have a grandmother and grandfather who loved her, and she would live in a normal home.

Cara's heart thudded loudly. *What is a normal home? And why is Marion making such a fuss about it? Jeremy is Jennifer's father; she's his daughter, and they deserve to have a home together. They will be a family, and Sharon would be a cherished memory.*

'I struggle to see why the Applicants think Jennifer would not have a normal home with her father,' Johnathon Gordon put to all present.

Marion promptly butted in. 'He is a single man. Who will mind her when he goes to work? What if he wants a new girlfriend? Will he still want Jennifer then? Will she accept Jennifer as her own? Or will she cramp his style?'

Cara noticed Jeremy bristle as he forced himself to remain seated.

'Who has been minding Jennifer this past year?' the Registrar asked, looking around the table.

'Not Jeremy,' Marion gloated.

'Who then? Not you?'

'No. *She* would not let me take her home with me.'

Cara remembered the visit before Christmas after Sharon's death. It had been pleasant until Marion began talking about taking Jennifer home with her. Jeremy had been back in the USA, his visa application in limbo. He'd gone through the process of changing Jennifer's birth certificate to include him as her father, so Marion had no legal rights to remove Jennifer.

'Who?'

'Her.' Marion pointed to Cara at the far end of the table. Cara was glad she was sitting as Marion had *that* look on her face, the look that blamed Cara. But Cara wasn't taking that blame anymore. She stared back at Marion, held her chin high and looked directly at her. Marion had always been a difficult person – demanding, Sharon had called her, unpredictable, some said – and sometimes it had seemed that Sharon could do no right. But she was Sharon's mother, and Cara trusted she loved Sharon in her own way. *So why is she doing this?*

The Registrar looked at Cara and then spoke quietly to the Family Consultant. Papers were passed around and studied while those sitting waited.

Cara kept her hands still as she was questioned: What was her name. Where did she live? And where did she work? And how did she come to be looking after Jennifer? These questions she answered easily and truthfully.

The Family Consultant asked Cara to look at a picture. It was one Jennifer had drawn: three circles with names written by an adult underneath. One had lines sticking out of the side, and it said Mimi; one with lines on the top said Mummy, and one that looked like two circles said Daddy.

'Who is Mimi?' Cara was asked.

'Jennifer calls me that.'

'Not mummy?'

'I'm not her mother.'

'She calls someone mummy – the pictures show someone called mummy.' The Family Consultant shuffled her papers.

'Sharon is her mother,' Cara stated. 'She passed away last year. We tell Jennifer that she got sick, and even though she wanted to stay with Jennifer, she had to go and be an Angel in heaven.

We hope she will understand one day.'

'We?'

'Jeremy, me … our friends.' Cara glanced around the table, her eyes resting on Jeremy.

'I see.' After a pause, she said, 'Do you have any questions, Mr Carter?''

He clasped his hands together on the table. 'Who minds Jennifer when you are working?'

'Liz, one day, and she goes to daycare for the other two days.'

'Who is Liz?'

Cara explained.

'How do you afford daycare and your mortgage working so few hours?'

Cara frowned. *What does this have to do with anything?* 'Jeremy helps with these things.' That was the truth.

'Are you in a sexual relationship with Jeremy Stonehouse?'

'No, why…?'

'Your Honour, what is the reason for this question?' Johnathon Gordon interjected.

'It brings into light the relationships that Jennifer is being exposed to,' Dixon Carter explained.

Cara glanced at Jeremy; he was boiling and struggling to keep calm. She looked into his eyes, tilted her head, and mouthed, 'It's okay.'

'Are you in a sexual relationship with David Hayle?' Dixon Carter asked next.

'Who …?'

'Surely you remember David Hayle, a married man with a child of his own. A married man you had an affair with.'

Cara gasped for breath. *David.* She wasn't having an affair with David. She loved David. She missed David and was waiting for David. Cara hadn't cried when David left, but now, she couldn't stop the tears from wetting her face. She rested her hand on the table and pushed her tears away with the other.

'I'm not … you don't know ….'

Jeremy pushed himself up from his chair, yelling. 'Stop it, leave her alone. Leave her alone.'

Cara gulped down her anguish, tried to remain calm, and let Jeremy know she was alright, to not do anything to jeopardise his chances.

'Leave her alone.' Jeremy fumed.

'Mr Gordon, control your client.'

Cara's head felt full of bees; she felt suddenly hot, and all the words seemed so far away, muffled by distance.

Then everything happened in slow motion. Johnathon Gordon tugged on Jeremy's sleeve and pulled him down to his seat. She saw Jeremy's head slump down to his chest, then he sat upright, and she heard him say, 'Let me visit Jennifer. You can take her if you let me visit.'

'No, Jeremy,' Cara cried. 'No.'

Reaching out, she grabbed his hand. He looked into her eyes, and she remembered the first time he'd done that. 'So long ago,' she whispered.

He smiled, but not the cheeky smile that had stirred her heart. He'd grown up over these past years. They all had.

'I'm sorry, Cara. I can't fight anymore; I can't let them do that to you.'

'I'm okay.'

'You're not.'

Cara saw Marion glance at Dixon Carter, a gloating snicker on her face.

'I will be. And you can't do this to Jennifer.' Cara ran her hand across her chest. She could not let this happen; she pulled back her distress, steadied her breathing and remembered David's face, and touch. *Loving you sucks, David Hayle*. She would wait.

'No!' The uneasy quiet was broken by Marion's husband, a tall, dark man with a Jamaican accent. He didn't address the court. He spoke directly to Marion. 'Do you never think why we didn't know about Jennifer? Why did our daughter not tell us she was pregnant? Why couldn't she tell us what was wrong with her before she died?'

'Mr Carter, I will not tolerate any more of this behaviour in my courtroom. Mr Gordon and Mr Stonehouse, you may stay. Everyone else is to leave this room immediately,' the Registrar stated.

Cara stumbled as she pushed her chair back, and Todd wrapped his arm around her; she glimpsed him nod his head to Jeremy as they left the room.

Outside in the hallway, Marion and her husband sat on a bench, staring blankly at each other. 'She's all I've got left....' Cara heard Marion plead.

'I know,' her husband said as he held her hand.

'What are we going to do?' Cara whispered mostly to herself. 'How can we fix this?'

Time passed.

'Cara …' Jeremy stood before her.

'What happened?'

The next day, Jennifer celebrated her third birthday with cake, sandwiches, and red cordial on the green lawn of Langley Park in front of Cara's apartment.

Brandon had sent her a parcel from the USA, and she sat on a blanket, ripping the paper as Cara tried to stop it from blowing into the river.

Inside was a box containing a Red Elmo doll from Sesame Street, a child's card and a note for Cara.

She knew a little about David's life from Jeremy but also knew she could not be in that life. David had to be a father to Brandon.

'Hey,' Jeremy said, indicating to a couple walking along the pathway beside the river, 'do you want to see them?' he asked Cara.

Cara stared at the couple heading towards her. She didn't understand what had happened in court yesterday. What did David have to do with Jeremy being Jennifer's father?

Todd said, 'I can ask them to leave. It's not appropriate for them to be here while the court still has to make its ruling.'

'No, it's Jennifer's birthday; they are her grandparents,' Jeremy said. 'Let them see her.'

Chapter Twenty-seven

Cara

Spring turned to summer.

In mid-December 1992, the court made its ruling. Jeremy was granted a visa for the court appearance. He had to provide proof of where Jennifer would live and where she would go to school, but his rights as Jennifer's biological father were recognised. Further orders granted visitation rights to Marion and her husband, as Jennifer's grandparents, by arrangement.

Christmas was spent on the riverbank to escape the sweltering heat, and then Jeremy returned to the USA, his visa having expired. Early in the new year, Jeremy asked Cara to join him and Jennifer when he took her home to the USA. She was granted a six-month visitor's visa and rented out her apartment.

***

Cara, Jeremy and Jennifer arrived in the USA on Valentine's Day, 1993. The first thing they did after recovering from the plane journey was take Jennifer to Pottery Barn.

Jeremy's apartment on Haight Street in San Francisco comprised five rooms, one used for living and dining, two bedrooms, a kitchen, and a bathroom. Jeremy had decorated the apartment with new wooden-looking flooring. He had painted the walls in the living area a light grey, but it was still a single man's home. The spare room was full of old gym and exercise equipment, and Golden State Warriors posters featuring Tim Hardaway were on the walls. The kitchen was in an alcove off the living room, with bits and pieces of crockery, cutlery and cookware.

After the trip to Pottery Barn, the spare room was painted pink and filled with furniture Jennifer had been allowed to choose. The bits and pieces in the kitchen were replaced with new and matching cutlery, crockery and cookware, and the bathroom had new towels. Jeremy insisted Cara have his room; he was sleeping on the pullout couch in the living room.

***

Four weeks after they arrived in San Francisco, Cara and David sat on a blanket at Baker Beach. Cara was close enough to know David was there, but far enough away to be acceptable.

'He's happy now,' David said.

His gaze followed Jeremy and Todd, their arms around each other as they watched Brandon and Jennifer clamber around on the black rocks that stood near the foot of the bridge. The love they shared had grown quickly, but they had kept it hidden in Perth. In San Francisco, a more open city, they did not. Even so, the paranoia around AIDS had wound its way into parts of this city; Baker Beach was not one of those places.

'Oh?'

David looked into Cara's eyes. 'I've always known how he feels, Cara. I love Jeremy. I always have. He is my friend.'

Cara wanted to reach for his hand, to hold his hand, to touch him, but she kept her distance, a respectable distance.

The ocean in the bay tossed white caps onto the pylons of the Golden Gate Bridge, its towers reaching into a sky shrouded in spring fog. Cara pulled her coat together. The warmth had gone as the day grew older, it was time to leave, but too soon to leave.

Cara was surprised the children seemed to remember each other as they were little more than babies. She was also surprised by how much of a mistake it was to think she could be with

David as *a respectable friend.* All her desperate efforts to remind herself that she was waiting for him, she was doing that. It was what she had promised to do, but she could not stop the fire from burning her soul.

She rubbed her hands together and ran them across her lips, watching the children climb in front of her. Climbing children are at risk, and Jennifer tripped and fell, crying. Cara went to help, but David placed his hand on her arm.

Cara shuddered, *his touch* through her coat. It was yesterday, the first time he'd run his fingers down her cheek. Her heart raced, and lightning spread through her body.

'How are we going to do this?' Cara turned to face David.

He brushed the tears from her cheek with the back of his fingers.

'We have to.' He pushed himself from the blanket and picked Brandon up.

Cara watched Jeremy hurry to Jennifer, frustration on his face when he bent to help her. He could not lift her, his strength had not completely recovered, and it might never. He shrugged Todd's hand off his shoulder as he brushed dirt from Jennifer's hands.

'You're okay. Are you hurt?' Jeremy asked.

Jennifer looked at him, sniffed and said, 'I'm okay, Daddy.'

Jeremy made his way to the blanket while Todd lifted Jennifer from the sand and sat her on Jeremy's knee, then he put his hand on his shoulder. Jeremy wound their fingers together, looked into Todd's eyes, and whispered, 'I'm sorry.'

Todd nodded.

'Alright?' Cara asked Jennifer.

'Daddy fixed it,' Jennifer said as she snuggled her head into Jeremy's shoulder.

Cara choked back her tears. 'Daddy did fix it.'

She wiped the tears from Jeremy's cheeks.

Chapter Twenty-eight

David

David sat opposite Alice in the dining room. She wore Versace blue jeans and a pink Baroque print jacket over a white t-shirt. Her hair was pushed behind her ears, but he could see the tiny lines under her eyes.

The antique mahogany table they shared was another addition to the house. He preferred to use the kitchen table, but Alice insisted on setting the dining table at least once a week so Brandon would learn. David was happy for Brandon to learn the lessons he would need as he grew into a man, but he wanted a balanced life for Brandon.

The Lexus parked in the garage was not a necessity, but it was a car David enjoyed driving, and he knew he was lucky to have it. He didn't want Brandon to grow up thinking he had entitlements, that things would fall into his lap. He wanted him to understand the value of working and money, as his parents had taught him.

Alice had never learnt these lessons. She was the only child of a wealthy couple, and perhaps they had tried to compensate for the time she spent without them.

Brandon was tucked in bed. He'd come home telling Alice about his afternoon with Jennifer, and David felt the anger boiling in her. Alice knew Jeremy and Cara had been in San Francisco for almost four weeks. Today was the first time the children had seen each other and the first time he'd seen Cara.

Cara was right: how were they going to see each other and keep up the pretence?

'I suppose you will be able to see her whenever you want now,' Alice said.

I can't do this anymore; it is a mistake to try.

He couldn't keep pretending; he did not want to continue this charade. Brandon was growing older and would soon notice the truth about him and Alice.

'I want a divorce.' He looked Alice in the eyes.

'You will not take Brandon.'

'You will not stop me from seeing him. I will fight you with everything I have.'

'Really, you think the courts will give you and the little slut custody. You will see Brandon only if I allow it.' Alice glared at him across the table. She'd always had what she wanted. Why would she think this would be any different?

He couldn't let her provoke him, so he slowed his breathing, swallowed and said, 'You don't love me, Alice. Why do you want me here? We haven't been intimate for more than two years.'

'Intimate! David, for fuck sake, how old are you! You sound like your grandfather. Intimate! Call it what it is, say it.'

The anger and hatred in her words didn't surprise him. He was trying to make a family for Brandon, but after Alice's lies and deception, he struggled with it. He was keeping a pretext up for Brandon.

'Call it what it is, David – it's sex, say it. Sex.' Alice sniggered. 'You think you will be able to have sex with the little whore whenever you want now, don't you? You won't have to wait until your next holiday so you can have sex with her, will you?'

David stared across the table. It wasn't hatred he saw in her eyes. It was possession. Alice wanted to control him. He was like a doll she'd grown tired of, put on a shelf so no one else could play with it. No longer wanted by her, but she would not let anyone else have it.

He pulled himself upright, squared his shoulders, and said, 'I do not have sex with Cara, I make love with her.'

The glass hit him in the temple. Wine splattered his face and his skin burned. Shards of glass mingled with blood, and blurred the vision in his right eye. He placed his hands on the table to steady himself and pushed himself upright.

'Where are you going?' Alice yelled.

'I'm getting Brandon, and we are leaving.' He forced himself away from the table and stumbled across the room. The world reeled around him, making it difficult to stand and concentrate, and blood in his eye made it difficult to see.

'You are not,' Alice screamed.

He heard the chair scrape the wooden parquet floor and her heels clattering as she stalked him across the dining room.

'Turn around and look at me.'

David reached out; blood ran down his cheek and dripped onto the floor. He grabbed the balustrade on the staircase, heaved himself upright and turned to face Alice.

'I'm ....'

The gun she held was not the one he kept in his study, the one he kept locked in the safe, with the bullets locked in another safe, in another room.

A mistake to try.

***

In the apartment on Haight Street, Cara staggered. She dropped the dish she was drying, and it fell to the tiled floor and shattered.

Cara stood staring at the broken pieces.

Jeremy rushed into the room.

'Cara!' He grabbed her arms.

Chapter Twenty-nine

David

David thought his eyes were open, but everything was dark. He tried to sit but could not move. 'Brandon, where is Brandon?' he managed to say.

'Brandon's with your mother ... where else would he be?'

Alice. It was Alice speaking to him, but it couldn't be.

'No, no.' David thrashed about in the bed, trying to move and get up. A hand rested on his shoulder.

'Darling, don't hurt yourself.'

'No.' The darkness around him grew deeper. He had to get out of here, and he had to find Brandon.

Darkness surrounded him.

The next time David opened his eyes, his vision was blurred. He was alone in a white room with tubes in his arms. When he tried to sit, pain forced him back onto the bed. *What had happened?* He remembered staring at a gun in Alice's hand, her anger and hatred, her words; *that little bitch is not having you.*

Nursing staff rushed into his room. The sounds he thought far away were the alarms on the machine attached to him.

'David ...' Someone was talking.

'What happened?' David mumbled.

'You've been shot.' It was a stranger talking, a doctor or a nurse. 'It's fortunate Alice came home when she did.'

'Alice?'

'She found you on the floor, called the ambulance, saved your life.'

'Alice?'

'Darling, I'm here,' Alice said. Sitting on his bed, she took his hand and pushed his hair away from his face.

'What happened?' David repeated.

'I don't know. The police think it was a robbery gone wrong,' Alice said.

Is this all a bad dream? The gun in her hands, the hatred in her words?

'Where's Brandon?'

'With your mother.'

Brandon's safe. 'Good.' He couldn't keep his eyes open; it was not right; something was not right. *Cara.*

Darkness swallowed him.

Cara

Cara sat on the step leading into Jeremy's apartment. She wrapped her arms around her knees and watched the taxi pull up at the curb and Jeremy alight. She wanted to stand, run to his arms, and find out, but couldn't move. He took the two steps up and sat beside her. Cara turned to face him.

'He's awake,' Jeremy said.

Cara gulped down her anguish and rested her hand on Jeremy's knee; he put his arms around her and said, 'Come in out of the cold; you are freezing.'

She looked into his eyes, 'Awake?'

'Yes.'

Jeremy helped Cara from the step, opened the front door, and sat her at the table in the living room. He popped his head into his daughter's bedroom, then made tea and placed the pot and cups on the table. Sitting opposite Cara, he poured the tea.

Cara warmed her hands on the cup, trying to stop the contents from spilling. 'Will he be …?' she asked.

'I hope so, Cara. I'm not family, and no matter how close we are, I can't get any information. I have to ask Alice.'

I'm not family.

'Jessica will have more information; I will ring her tomorrow. You should try and rest now.'

Jeremy had come home from his Saturday morning basketball game ashen and shaking, saying Jessica had called him at eleven-thirty that morning, telling him David had been seriously wounded at home last night. It was nearly midnight now.

Cara placed her cup on the table and buried her head in her hands, pushing back her tears.

'Come on, let's get to bed. There is nothing we can do tonight,' Jeremy said.

He put his arms around Cara and helped her from the chair. She leaned into his warm body, and he offered shelter. She said, 'Don't sleep on the couch tonight; stay with me.'

'I'll stay with you,' he said. Then he said, 'David will be alright.'

'Yes,' Cara whispered.

The next morning, Cara woke to the sound of children chattering and the smell of coffee brewing. She pulled her blue velour robe from the back of the bedroom door and dragged it over her shoulders before opening it. Cara checked the other bedroom and saw Jennifer and Brandon playing with blocks.

She could hear Jeremy clattering around in the kitchen. Jessica sat at the kitchen table, coffee and pastries untouched. The man sitting opposite her could only be David's father. Cara ran her hands through her tangled hair, unsure of her place in the tableau. No one looked like they'd had much sleep during the night.

'Do you want some coffee?' Jeremy asked as he came out of the kitchen.

Cara nodded. 'Please.'

As she entered the room, David's parents stood to greet her. Jessica pulled her into her arms and held her tight, then introduced Cara to Robert Hayle. He extended his hand, and Cara shook it. He did not approve or disapprove of her; his handshake told her that.

Jeremy poured coffee and sat on the empty chair at the table. 'I can't get any information from the hospital,' he said.

'We went early this morning. David is stable, still serious, but stable,' Robert said.

'Will he be alright?' Cara murmured.

Jessica took Cara's hand and said firmly, 'Yes.' She looked across the table at her husband, her eyes determined.

'What happened?' Jeremy asked.

'Alice says she came home and found David on the floor. The doctors are not sure, his injuries are confusing. He's been struck in the face by a glass object, and he could have some damage to his right eye. Luckily, the gunshot missed any major organs.' Robert sounded like he was giving a news report.

'Brandon?'

'He was home with David when this all happened. Thank goodness he was not hurt; he might have seen something, but he is too young to articulate,' Robert said. 'The police want a child specialist to speak to him, but Alice has refused to allow this. We agree with her, he is too young and too upset to have to be put through such a thing.'

'Come and get some fruit,' Jeremy called the children.

He had set a blanket on the floor in front of the television and put fruit and juice in the middle.

'Coming, Daddy,' Jennifer said as she and Brandon entered the living room.

'Daddy hurt,' Brandon said.

Jessica stood, picked him up and carried him back to the chair. 'Yes, Daddy's hurt, but he is getting better in the hospital.'

Jeremy scooped Jennifer from the floor and sat her on his knee.

'Mummy hurt,' Brandon said.

'No,' Jessica said. 'Mummy's not hurt.'

'No, no, no,' Brandon said, pounding his fists into Jessica's chest. 'Mummy hurt Daddy,' he cried.

Jessica grasped her grandson's hands together and held him as he sobbed; she ran her hands through his hair trying to comfort him.

The adults at the table sat staring at the little boy in his grandmother's arms, the words he'd spoken creating a silent, frozen chasm broken only by his sobs.

Cara was back in Austria. Alice leaning forward, her face close to Cara's, her blue eyes, cold steel. *David is mine, he has always been mine and will always be mine. You will not take him away from me.*

Chapter Thirty

Cara

The next day Cara was back on the steps of Jeremy's apartment; he had taken Jennifer to spend time with Brandon.

The March sun warmed her face, and she watched the world go by: cars cruising up and down the hilly street, people walking and jogging, dogs barking, and on the wind amongst the sounds of the traffic, boat whistles—all normal sounds of a busy port city. The unease surrounding her threatened to engulf her. She pushed at it, but what the little boy said yesterday ate at her. Had Brandon misread what he saw? What had Alice done?

The post was delivered by hand where she was making her home, and she stood to greet the postman, who handed her a letter postmarked Perth, Western Australia, dated March 3rd, 1993.

A letter from Liz.

> *Dear Cara,*
>
> *I hope everything is going okay in the USA. Mike and I are busy as always and we have very wonderful news. I am finally pregnant. We have waited until now to let everyone know our baby is due towards the middle of August.*
>
> *I hope Jennifer is settling in with her Daddy. It's funny we say all the words, but until it's your turn to be a parent, you don't understand what you are saying. Please tell me you would be happy to be*

our baby's godmother, there is no one else I would consider asking.

I have been well, just some early morning sickness that lasted a few weeks, so I am very lucky.

I have enclosed a letter that was sent to your apartment, it's from Dublin. I presume it is news from your grandparents.

Love

Liz xxx

My grandparents? Cara still held those secrets close – maybe one day she could tell Liz. But now, only David knew the truth, and he was lying in a hospital, and she couldn't see him, hold him, or touch him. She had to wait for secondhand information.

Frowning as her fingers ripped the envelope, Cara shook her head. She didn't know anyone in Dublin.

The letter was dated 16th February 1993.

Dear Miss Maloney,

My name is Briget Aherne. I am sorry to hear about Father Francis Kelly's death in August last year. He had been in touch with me in the past about the Magdalen Laundry in High Park, Dublin, a facility I have been investigating as a journalist.

Father Kelly told me that you are seeking information about your mother, Margaret Rose Maloney, who was sent to Ireland in 1964, not long after you were born. I am afraid I have not had much success in this matter, and I am sure Father Kelly told you all he could.

156

I wish to let you know that the Sisters are selling land that holds a graveyard at High Park. When the application for exhumation was presented on August 6, 1992, the Sisters were advised that they would need to identify all the women buried there before any further steps could be taken. Death certificates were requested, for all the bodies before they could be removed and reburied. Another application was presented on January 28, 1993.

I am hopeful I will be able to obtain further information about those buried, and I will let you know if I find any record of your mother.

So many of these poor women were abandoned by their families, and I am heartened that you are searching for your mother. I will do all I can to help you with your search.

I have included my details so you can contact me.

God bless you,

Briget

Cara wiped her tears away. Her mother: Cara might never know where she was or what had happened to her. If she was alive, wouldn't she have had contact? But Cara remembered the old building at High Park. The graves on the lawn, the old Nun, her memory broken, shuffling in front of her. If her mother had survived, would she remember Cara?

Cara ran her hands through her hair, her stomach churning. She had to do something. She couldn't sit on this step anymore. She didn't know where David was or where he lived.

Her frustration threatening to boil over, she pushed herself up from the step as a grey car pulled up at the curb in front of her. Two men stepped out. Cara's eyes darted along the street; she didn't know these men.

'Cara Maloney?' one queried as he pulled something from his pocket.

'Miss Maloney, my name is Detective Peter Nugent.'

She stared at the badge in his hand. How would she know if was real or not?

***

Cara sat on a chair behind a wooden table with two men opposite her. She'd been allowed to make a phone call, so she called Jeremy. She was in a scene from a rerun of *The Streets of San Francisco*. Detective Nugent was a craggy older man, his grey suit pulling at his belly and his skin burnt from the sun, he even wore a hat. The other man was younger, clean-shaven, with short dark hair slicked back He wore a leather jacket over a black t-shirt and fitted jeans.

Like a deer in a headlight, unable to move, unable to think, Cara stared at the dull beige walls, the only light coming from one bulb in the ceiling. She didn't understand the words spoken until she heard 'David Hayle.'

She shook her head. 'What ... who?'

'Do you know a man named David Hayle? What is your relationship with him?'

'David ... I ...,' Cara began to giggle.

'Do you think this is funny, Miss Maloney?'

How can this be anything other than a joke? Brandon had seen what happened, although that was too hard to believe, and now she was being questioned by the police about David.

'Alice ....'

'Don't say anything else, Cara,' Todd said as he came into the room.

'Mr Ledowski,' Detective Nugent said. 'This is not your normal area of practice. Aren't you the Hayle family lawyer? Is this one of your Pro Bono cases?'

'I am David Hayle's lawyer, and Miss Maloney is my client.'

Todd put his briefcase on the desk next to Cara and rested his hand on her shoulder, he turned her to face him and repeated. 'Don't say anything else, I am here to help you. Detective Nugent, what is my client being questioned about?' Todd asked as he sat on the chair next to Cara.

'Alice Hayle has given us your client's name as a person of interest in the attempted murder of her husband. She says they had an affair when he was in Australia in August last year and suggested your client was jealous that he had returned to be with her.'

An affair, when will our relationship be anything more than a tawdry affair? Cara shook her head. She loved David, and he loved her. He stayed with Alice only for Brandon; surely Alice wouldn't go to such lengths. Brandon's words, *No, No, No, Mummy hurt Daddy,* slammed into her mind.

'Where was your client on Friday 12th March at 9.00 pm.'

'Todd,' Cara quizzed.

'My client was at home.'

'Alone?'

'No, with Jeremy Stonehouse, who is making a statement at this moment.' Todd stood and said, 'Unless you have any further questions, we are leaving.'

'Nothing at the moment. Miss Maloney must make herself available if we need to speak to her again.'

'Of course.'

Chapter Thirty-one

David

David did not know how long he had been in the hospital bed. He was clean-shaven and remembered being washed and having his hair combed; he wore a hospital gown. His eye was bandaged, and painkillers eased the pain there and in his chest and shoulder.

He remembered Alice holding his hand; a heartbroken wife, and he knew that was wrong. He did not know why that was wrong, but he knew it was.

Alice walked through the door, blonde ponytail swishing, her heels clicking on the linoleum floor. He was back in the dining room of his home. His mind fogged then filled: the room full of shadows. He felt glass strike his face and heard himself say, *I'm getting Brandon, and we are leaving.*

Alice sat on the bed beside him and took his hand, her touch, his skin crawled. *Why does her touch make me wince?*

'What do you remember?' There was no gentleness, no kindness in those words; they were alone, and Alice wanted to know what he recalled.

David pulled his hand away and pushed himself upright in the bed. *What did he remember?* He was getting Brandon and leaving. *Why? A burglary gone wrong?* That wasn't right. Alice holding a gun; Brandon screaming at the top of the staircase. Pain and darkness.

'Good to see you sitting up,' Dr Donna Arden said as she came into the room. She took the chart from the end of his bed and studied the notes.

'Darling, do you remember?' Alice gushed, fussing with his hair. She turned to the doctor, 'He doesn't seem to remember; will he be alright.' Tears fell down her cheeks, and she pushed them away.

'These things take time. Trauma can often affect the memory.'

'Darling, I'm here. Don't worry, I will help you remember.' Her voice trembled as she turned back to the doctor. 'What can I do?'

'Just be there for David. He will remember when he's ready.'

Alice reached for his hand, he couldn't pull it away, why did he want to? She was his wife, Brandon's mother.

Brandon. He remembered: Brandon screaming at the top of the stairs. The fog moved. Searing pain, his face covered in blood and pieces of glass. Staggering across the floor, leaning on the balustrade. Alice holding a gun. He remembered Alice holding a gun … *that little bitch is not having you.*

Cara.

***

David sat holding his son close, keeping his pain to himself. He ruffled Brandon's hair as he curled into his chest before sitting up, his eyes wide. The hand he reached out trembled as it hovered near the bandage on David's eye.

'It's okay,' David said. 'Daddy will be a pirate now.' He tried to make a pirate voice, but the painkillers let him down; still, it seemed enough to calm Brandon.

'Mummy hurt,' Brandon said.

What could David say? He remembered what had happened, but Alice was Brandon's mother; he had to believe she would never do anything to hurt him. He looked over Brandon's head to Jessica, sitting on the chair beside the bed.

'Brandon's been staying with Poppa and Nannie; Mummy's been busy visiting Daddy and arranging the parade for today,' Jessica said.

St Patrick's Day parade down Market Street. The store had floats and sponsored several other events on the day, a celebration of all things Irish in the city of San Francisco.

Jessica lifted Brandon off David's bed, sat him on her knee, and kissed his forehead. David let out a breath he didn't know he was holding; Brandon was safe.

'Mummy?' Brandon said.

'Daddy fell down,' David said.

The little boy cocked his head, 'Daddy hurt?'

'Yes, Daddy got hurt.'

Brandon would be three on his next birthday, in April, and David hoped the memory of what he had seen would fade.

Jessica ruffled Brandon's hair and said, 'Shall we go and see the parade ... see what Mummy's been doing?'

'Daddy will listen from here; I will hear the music through the window. I hope you don't get wet in the rain.'

Brandon slipped from his grandmother's knee and stood beside the bed, and David lifted him onto his chest again, his eyes dimming as his chest exploded. *Brandon must not know.*

'Come on, let's go and see the parade.' Jessica lifted Brandon from the bed, stood him on the floor and took his hand.

'Can you find your way home?' Jessica asked as she left the room.

'Yes,' Cara replied.

Cara

Cara collapsed onto the chair beside the bed. She could see David sucking air in, the arm he'd kept hidden from Brandon had tubes running from his elbow to his wrist connected to a drip and other machines beside the bed. The tears she promised

162

herself she would not shed, spilled over and ran down her cheeks. David reached out, and she took his hand. He seemed to have used all his energy and closed his eyes. Cara leaned forward, touching her forehead to his. She felt fingers run down her cheek, and she sat upright to see David had his eyes open.

'Hey,' he whispered. The hand that had stroked her cheek fell to the bed, and the alarms on the machine bellowed. Medical staff rushed into the room, moving Cara aside. She stood slumped against the wall, chewing her fingers, watching.

Monitors checked; pulse taken, claret threads winding through the hospital robe he wore. David lay motionless.

***

Gentle fingers weaved through Cara's hair, she lifted her head from her folded arms on David's bed, and the pain in his brown eyes sliced through her.

'Hey,' she said.

When he tried to speak, she put her finger to his lips and said, 'Hush.' Cara pushed back her tears. 'I can't stay: the nurse called Alice.'

David caught her hand. 'Don't go.'

'I ....' Cara ran her finger across his lips. 'I have to go.'

Cara could hear voices in the hallway and heels clacking on the floor. She dragged her hand away and hurried to the door. Pushing it open, she saw Alice with the medical staff at the nurse's station. Cara dashed down the hallway and around a corner before she was seen.

***

Cara stood kicking water around with her bare feet. The pink water reflected the setting sun, and the evening sky shone orange and yellow. Traffic noise rumbled in the air, and lights from the vehicles shone, creating fairy lights running along the bridge.

She found comfort in the ocean; the water was icy, but a touch of eucalyptus mingled in the pine-scented air at Baker Beach. That had been a surprise to see eucalyptus trees around the streets of San Francisco, and Cara would linger beneath them, taking in the scent when she longed for her country.

St Patrick's Day seemed to be celebrated much the same, though, parades, singing, dancing and copious amounts of alcohol to share. Street drinking appeared to be overlooked on this day, much as it was at home. Revellers were either in high spirits, singing ditties or weeping over some tragic Irish ballad. She'd shrugged off unwanted attention from a group of young men who commented on her Irish appearance, her red curls and green eyes, and her strange accent. Why was she all alone on this special Irish day? They had been harmless, but Cara was pleased when the mounted police rode by, and they scurried away.

'Cara,' Jeremy called. She turned to see him coming across the sand. The drizzle turned to rain. 'Come on, you're getting wet.' He wrapped the blanket he carried around her shoulders. 'It's rough here, you could get swept off your feet, the rips are strong.'

'I can swim.'

'Not here, you can't. People have been swept away by unexpected waves.'

He steered her away from the water, picked up her shoes and helped her across the sand to a beach shelter.

'David?'

'He's all good. Too much excitement busted his stitches. But he is okay.'

'Oh, Jeremy, what can I do?'

Jeremy folded her in his arms, and Cara wept. She sobbed fully, letting herself cry as Jeremy held her. Then she pulled out of his arms, wiped her face, put her shoes on and said, 'Let's go home.'

David

Two weeks later, David left the hospital. He went home with his devoted wife and child to the house on Buchanan Street in Pacific Heights, his arm in a sling and a patch over his right eye.

On the 10th of April, Easter Saturday, Brandon celebrated his third birthday. Alice arranged a birthday party more suitable for a 21st than a 3rd birthday with family and friends. When David tired of the festivities, he sat on the balcony looking over the rooftops and across the water to the other side of the bay.

He must take Brandon and leave. It was difficult to understand what had happened that day, perhaps he shouldn't have pushed Alice like he did. She had always wanted all his attention when they were children, he just thought it was what girls did, being only a child himself. But he was a man now and would protect himself and Brandon. As far as Alice knew, he did not remember what had happened, and he would keep it that way.

David turned as the sliding door opened, and his grandfather stepped onto the balcony. At eighty-five, a stick helped him stand straight, his dark hair was almost white now, but his brown eyes and sharp mind seemed to notice what others missed. He sat on the other chair on the balcony, reached out, and patted David on the knee.

'It's been a while since we've talked,' he said. 'How are you doing?'

'I'm good, Grandad.' His eye was no longer patched, and his arm was out of the sling. 'The plastic surgeon expects the scars to fade, and my sight is improving.'

'David?'

'I didn't understand, Grandad. I shouldn't have pushed her.'

'Don't, David. You don't take the blame for someone else's actions, only take the blame for your actions, you know that.'

'Yes.' He knew that.

'I have to believe Alice won't hurt Brandon, but I can't now. What happens if she has too much to drink? I have to be here to protect him.'

'Yes, you must protect Brandon, but you don't have to stay here.'

'I do. I will lose custody of him if I don't.'

'And Cara?'

'Cara will not come between Brandon and his mother, Grandad.'

Heels clacked on the tiled balcony, and David swung around. How long had Alice been listening?

Chapter Thirty-two

Cara

Cara received a letter dated 15th April 1993.

Dear Cara-Rose, it read.

> *I hope you are well, and thank you for your current address.*

> *My investigations into High Park have led to disturbing discoveries, but I believe you will want to know these details.*

> *I have learnt that when the exhumation application for the bodies in the graveyard at High Park was presented on 28th January 1993, only 75 of the bodies could be identified by name. There are 56 unidentified bodies. 30 have no death certificates or cause of death. Others were identified by pseudo-religious names, but there is one body identified by her first name. That name is Rose. I do not want to distress you, but I thought you would like to know.*

> *The science of DNA testing might be able to determine if there is any connection between you and Rose. I have included an address in San Francisco where you can have these tests done if that is something you wish to do. The results could be sent to Ireland to be checked when her body is exhumed if we can get permission from the church.*

I do not have a date for the exhumation. The application is being considered but there is no certainty and no way of knowing when it will be approved.

The records that have been left undone date from 1942 to 1968. Not having death certificates for these women is considered criminal in Ireland.

I am sorry, it seems such a distant hope and I wish I could offer you more.

God bless you,

Briget

Cara handed the letter to David. They sat together under a striped umbrella on a sunny day, drinking coffee and eating ice cream sundaes. Cara could see glimpses of the ocean at Fisherman's Wharf. Seabirds squawked and squabbled over scraps; boat whistles hung in the air and the day's catch floated on the breeze surrounding them.

It was Monday, the 3rd of May. Jeremy and Alice were at work, and the children were at preschool. David asked her to meet him in a public place, and Cara did not say no. She had not seen him since St Patrick's Day, in the hospital; the day she fled from Alice. His blue t-shirt, under a light blue denim jacket tucked into cream chinos, seemed too big for him. He no longer gelled his hair, and it blew across his dark sunglasses, which did not hide the scar running down the right cheek of his pale face. He looked up from the letter, reached across the table and wiped the tears from her cheeks. Cara shuddered.

'I'm sorry,' he said. 'I will come with you if you want to do the test.'

'Mmm, I'm ....' Cara shook her head, she wasn't sure. 'Maybe,' she said.

It was too much to think about, and she wanted to spend this precious time with David. She reached out and touched the scar on his face with the back of her fingers.

'It's okay,' he said.

She took his hands and clutched them tight. 'It's not.'

How could Alice have done this? There was no doubt that Alice had done this. David kept it close. Brandon's words, as unbelievable as they were, were the only evidence, and those words were kept close by those who'd heard them.

There was no evidence of a break-in at his home. The injuries to David's face could only have been from a glass or bottle hitting him. The gunshot could have been the result of a burglary, but nothing had been stolen, and the house had not been ransacked. It was Alice who had suggested a burglary gone wrong, and it was Alice who had suggested Cara could be a suspect.

'You can't stay there with her.' Cara's fingers wiped away the pressure under her eyes. She was not going to cry.

'I know, but I can't leave, not yet. I have to stay with Brandon.' David smiled gently as he watched her brush her cheeks.

'You need to be safe to do that.'

He reached out and took her hand. 'She won't do anything again.' Cara knew what David was saying – he was telling her he knew the words Brandon had spoken were true. She controlled her fear and sucked in a breath. Brandon had to be safe, David had to do that.

'Let's not talk about her … let's go for a walk,' he said.

The wind blew the bottom of Cara's A-line white floral embossed summer dress around her knees. She held David's hand as they walked down Larkin Street to the waterfront. Sand filled their shoes, and cold water tickled their toes. For lunch, they ate chowder at a restaurant on a jetty overlooking the bay before a cable car and taxi took them to Cara's front door.

A door she thought was safe.

***

A key in the lock woke Cara. She grabbed her robe from the back of her bedroom door, left and pulled the door shut behind her. Pushing tangled hair away from her face, she said, 'What time is it?'

'Just after two.' Jeremy laughed, and a smile ran across his face.

'I have to get Jennifer.'

'I'll get Jennifer.' He backed out of the doorway, put his hand on the frame and said, 'We will have dinner at Todd's tonight.'

He grinned, and his eyes sparkled – he knew who was in the bedroom because there could only be one person in the bedroom. Jeremy pulled the door shut, and Cara heard the key lock. She leaned her head against the bedroom door before opening it.

David lay sleeping peacefully; a peaceful sleep she doubted he'd had in a long time. The bullet wound on his right shoulder had brought tears to her eyes. She did not understand, but she did remember Alice in Austria, remembered the hate. It seemed Alice would rather David be dead if she did not control him. Cara had to stop that.

She pulled the sheet back and climbed into bed beside him, and he opened his eyes. 'Hi,' he said.

She kissed his mouth and felt him stir. She pushed the sheets down and knelt over his body, running her fingers along the inside of his thigh. He breathed deeply as she bent her head and followed her fingers with her mouth. He shuddered as her hands and mouth enjoyed his body. She wrapped herself around him and pulled him deep into her as she straddled him. Cara sat upright until she could no longer hold herself, and she fell forward, burying her face in his chest.

David held her tight, so tight she thought she would break, but he knew his strength and loosened his grip on her. He caressed her shoulders and back as her breathing became less erratic and her heartbeat returned close to normal. Cara snuggled into David's chest and listened to his heartbeat as she slipped into a gentle sleep.

David

David opened the door to his home. His father sat at the dining table, and he could hear crockery clattering around in the kitchen.

'Coffee?' his mother called as she came from the kitchen to the dining room, coffee pot in hand.

David nodded. 'Thank you.'

Then he asked, 'Brandon?'

'In bed asleep.'

Nancy would pick Brandon up from Kindy, which was his arrangement with her, she would wait until he came home before finishing her work for the day. David was usually home before 4 pm, but today he was late, and he could not and would not hide the reason. He had called his mother.

'Is Alice home?'

'Upstairs,' Jessica said.

'David, you have to ….'

'Not now, Dad.'

He didn't want to do this now. He had just had a day he never thought he would, and the joy of Cara's lovemaking still clung to the fibres of his being. Her scent still lingered on his body, and he wanted to enjoy it.

Jessica poured three cups of coffee, and David sat at the table with his parents.

'What time …?'

'Alice came home about half an hour ago.'

Alice had started staying back for drinks after work with her single colleagues. Sometimes, they would drink until the early hours and then she would be up and dressed for work the following day, but she was getting sloppy and was beginning to make mistakes.

He knew how important the Italian designer was to Alice. He also knew the Italian designer demanded exceptional attention to detail. David had already smoothed over an invoicing error for one of the store's most prestigious customers.

As he remembered the day he'd had with Cara, he shook himself; *I'm not doing this anymore.*

'We need to talk, Dad,' he said.

The next morning Alice came down to breakfast. Brandon was at kindy school, and David sat at the kitchen table working with his laptop, an IBM ThinkPad that would allow him to work wherever he was. *Why?*

'Why didn't you wake me?' Alice demanded. Running her hands through her hair, pushing sticky blonde hair from her face, blinking mascara-clumped eyelashes, rubbing the discoloured blush from her cheeks. She wore her slip and underwear, her feet bare, a silk robe falling off her shoulders.

He looked up from the computer screen. *Why have I waited so long?*

'Where's Brandon?'

'He's at school, as you know.'

'I will be late for work.'

'I have called you in sick today.'

'What … why?' Alice fell onto the chair opposite him, her hand shaking as she poured coffee.

'Look at yourself.'

The contempt in Alice's eyes as she glared at him might have worried him once, but not now.

'You can't do that?'

'It's done. Angelo will not accept you turning up for work late and like this.'

'Daddy, won't let you do this to me?'

'Daddy, can't stop me.'

David pushed himself from the table, shut the computer, and turned to leave. She scraped her chair as she stumbled from the table.

'You can't do this.' Alice chased him across the room, grabbed his arm, and stopped him.

He turned to face her. 'Don't. Brandon and I will be leaving. There is no reason for us to stay here any longer.'

'I'm his mother! You will not take him away from me.'

'You haven't put Brandon first for a long time. Not like a mother should.'

Alice raised her fists to strike him, but he grabbed her wrists. 'Go and have a shower; you reek of alcohol.'

David let her wrists loose, turned, and walked away. The last time he'd turned his back on Alice, she had almost killed him, and his legs trembled as he made his way up the stairs and into his study. He locked the door and staggered to his desk, taking deep breaths.

Chapter Thirty-three

Cara

Cara tried not to cry at the words Briget had written; she had only seen kindness once in her search for her mother, so she had not expected any other decision about the DNA test, but it was a hope to cling to.

> *Dear Cara,*
>
> *I hope you are well, and thank you for your letter.*
>
> *It is a big step to take the DNA test, and I commend your courage for doing this. Unfortunately, I am unable to get permission from the sisters to match your DNA with Rose. I will continue to seek their permission, and maybe there will be a change of heart by the time the results are available.*
>
> *The wall of silence continues, and even though the sisters have a chance to make things right for you, they do not seem to have the will or the compassion to do this. I am sorry, I do not want to build up your hopes as the chances of them changing their ruling are remote.*
>
> *I have been told a further exhumation application was made around 12 May 1993, and I believe the licence to exhume was granted two*

weeks later. This is now going out to tender.

I do not have any further information, but I will continue following this story and hope to get answers for you.

God Bless You

Briget

Cara folded the letter and placed it on the kitchen table. She had shopping to do before picking Jennifer up from preschool. Cara had insisted on helping around the flat, as she was unable to work without a green card. Her return ticket to Australia was booked, with her visa due to expire on 14th August 1993.

Cara shuddered at that thought. She would miss Jennifer, but Jennifer was happy and settling with Jeremy, and Todd was part of that life. Jeremy had arranged for Marion and her husband to visit during the summer school holidays, which would start next week.

Cara had not seen David since the day they'd shared almost a month ago. He stayed in the house he shared with Alice, making a home for Brandon. The gnawing in her body swamped her.

The knock on the door startled her and made her jump in her seat. She was not expecting anyone. Jeremy was at work, and he had his key, and the post had been delivered.

David stood at the door. 'Hey.'

Cara fell into his arms, lifting her head seeking his mouth, tasting him, consuming him. She pushed herself out of his arms. He seemed stronger, the scar on his face cut into her heart, but his eyes devoured her. Cara threw herself back into his arms, and he scooped her from the floor and pushed the door shut with his foot. She wrapped her legs around his back as he carried her into the apartment.

'I have to pick up ....'

'I know. I just needed to see you.' He sat on the couch, and pushed her hair away from her face as she curled into his body. And she needed to see him, touch him, be with him. Cara pulled his face to hers and chewed his lips, exploring his mouth, letting him explore her mouth. 'I have to ...,' she mumbled.

Pulling herself away, she sat on his lap and ran her fingers through his hair, down the scar on his face and across his lips.

'I miss you,' he said.

'Me too.' She pushed herself reluctantly from his knees. 'Can you come for a walk.'

David nodded and she took his hand as she pulled the front door closed. They walked slowly down Haight Street to be together for a time.

Cara waited in front of the school with the other parents. She could taste David's kiss and ran her fingers across her lips, savouring that memory of his mouth on hers. Even though it was summer, Cara wore a windcheater over her jeans and t-shirt. Her curls blew around her face, and she kept her sunglasses on as she stood on Grove Street waiting for the school doors to open.

Jennifer ran into her arms as she entered the building, chattering about her day at school and asking if her new friend from today could come home with her. This was a daily event, and Cara smiled and nodded but made excuses that mostly appeased Jennifer. Today she promised a visit with Brandon. Jennifer squealed and jumped into her arms.

The following Sunday, the first in June, as Cara and David walked together, she slipped her hand into his as they wandered along behind Jeremy and Todd, who held hands as Jennifer and Brandon raced around up the hilly slopes to Buena Vista Park playground. As they crested the hill, Cara's hat blew off her head and, racing down the hill after it, she stomped her foot on the rim to stop it from running away. Cara bent to pick up the hat and David placed his hand over hers, pulling her into his arms. His lips were warm and sweet from the ice cream they had shared. He wrapped her in his arms as they trudged up the hill, removing his arms when in sight of the playground.

The playground was deserted, and the children had the slides and swings to themselves. Jeremy rested his hand on Todd's knee as they sat together, but Cara and David sat apart, always aware of Brandon.

Chapter Thirty-four

Cara

Cara stared at the words on the paper, but they didn't change. She sat on the front step of Jeremy's flat, squinting in the summer sun, gulping in breath, and letting her tears fall.

My dear Cara,

The information I have is distressing, but I hope it will give you comfort.

I was able to speak to an elderly sister from High Park, and she has a memory of a young sister returning from overseas, as she said, in the 60s. It is a long time ago and the elderly sister has only bits and pieces of a memory. A memory of a young woman surrounded by sadness and melancholy who cried herself to sleep most nights. This young woman faded from the old woman's memory as the years went by.

The records from High Park that I have seen mentioned the return of a sister from Western Australia in 1964. There is a further mention of this young sister when she passed away two years later, it was noted that she was buried with the name Rose on her grave. The evidence suggests that Rose is your mother, but I am unable to get permission from the sisters to match your DNA test with her.

I am so very sorry to give you this news, and I will continue searching for further proof if you would like me to do this. You must continue your life as you have done, I am sure your mother would want that for you, and I am sure she loved you.

Ireland's involvement in these Laundries is a blight on the soul of our nation. I hope one day we will make amends and there will be justice for the women incarcerated in these institutes. Until then, we will continue to knock on the wall.

God bless you.

Briget

The letter was dated 10th June 1993.

***

Cara rubbed her chest and wiped her cheeks with the back of her hand as a taxi pulled up in the street in front of her. David jumped out, ran across the path, up the step, and sat beside her, pulling her into his arms.

'I love you, Cara,' he whispered.

She pushed herself out of his arms. 'They knew,' she said, running her hand across her shoulder, across the scar that had been there for almost twenty years. 'All this time, they knew.'

'They can't hurt you anymore.'

She lowered her head to David's chest and listened to the heartbeat of the man she loved, the man who loved her.

A lifetime of hope, longing, and yearning withered as white clouds floated in a blue sky. Traffic rolled up and down the hilly road, and the world went on around her.

Chapter Thirty-five

David

On the 4th of July, Independence Day, San Francisco celebrated with fireworks and a long weekend.

David sat watching the sun make its way toward the horizon, splashing gold and orange through the trees into a lake. Jeremy and Todd paddled a canoe, with Jennifer and Brandon hanging over the sides, running their fingers in the water.

He held Cara's hand as she sat beside him on the back step of the family's cabin near Mill Valley. Cara was in his life; he wanted her in his life; he was over pretending she wasn't, and he was over keeping up the pretence with Alice.

He wasn't doing that anymore.

He turned to face Cara and said, 'I'm filing for divorce and seeking custody of Brandon. Todd will work it out, but I want him to wait until you leave.'

Until you leave … how will I say goodbye to you again?

'Alice can't do anything to me,' Cara said.

She looked into his eyes, and he remembered the first day he'd done that, the first day he'd drowned in those emerald pools. They'd been apart for so long, but she was here with him now.

'No, Cara,' he said firmly. He knew how Alice would drag Cara into any court case, but it was more than that. For some reason he needed Cara to be away from Alice. He didn't understand why he had this feeling – it ate at him – he knew Cara had to be away from Alice.

'Once it's over, we can be together,' he said.

Cara squeezed his hand. 'Yes.'

'I love you and want you in my life.'

'I know.' Cara ran her fingers down the scar on his face.

He had to wait until Cara left. He had to say goodbye to her again. But not yet, he would take the days he had and be with her when he could.

The children's voices echoed off the water, and Cara returned their waves. She turned back to him and asked. 'How is Alice going in the program?'

'She seems to be doing alright. It's been ten days; she seems to be getting help.'

'That is good for Brandon.'

He turned his face away, stood from the step, and walked down the pathway under overhanging tree branches to the water's edge. Cara followed him and turned his face to her.

'What?'

'She's not doing it for Brandon ….' He sucked up his words. 'I hoped he might be important enough, but ...'

Cara wiped the tears from his cheeks.

'She's doing it for Angelo – she went to work hungover, and he sent her home. She was livid, but her father took Angelo's side. That was a shock for Alice. To think she might lose her job, it's important to her.'

There had been another fight after that. But the thought of losing her position with the Italian designer had been enough for Alice to seek help at Tranquillity Ridge, a clinic in the hills of San Francisco where she was attending a 30-day program. He had to believe Alice loved Brandon – she was his mother – but she was not attending the program for him. She was doing it for herself. His little boy wasn't important enough, but some good might come out of it, and Brandon would get the benefit one day.

181

David lowered his head, not wanting Cara to see his tears, but she tilted his chin and said, 'I'm sorry.'

Cara

Cara sat with fireflies floating in the dark sky around her, something she had never seen before. Brandon and Jennifer watched sparks rise into the sky as they toasted marshmallows on sticks over an open firepit. Jeremy and Todd sat with their arms wrapped around each other, keeping watch, *just like in the movies*. David sat on one side of the firepit, and Cara sat on the other, away from each other.

'Bedtime soon,' David said.

'Aww, not yet,' the children said in unison.

'Soon.'

David left the children in Jeremy's care and wandered down to the dark water's edge. He carried a torch to light the path, and Cara followed him. In the dark of night, she put her arms around his neck and pulled him close.

'Sleep with me tonight?' he asked.

Cara tilted her head back to look up at him. 'Brandon?'

'The children can sleep in the bunk room tonight.'

'Will they be … safe?'

'It's all enclosed and the only entry door is from my room, I'm sure they will love it.'

The cabin was bigger than Cara expected. She thought it would be one room where everyone bunked down together. David told her that was what it used to be like, but over the years, it had been extended by his grandparents and then his parents. Now there were two bedrooms and the bunkroom, where he'd spent his time as a child. The living area was original, with timber-lined walls and ceilings and a fireplace. The bathroom was still out the back on the porch, but the kitchen was inside and had been updated.

In the bedroom, Cara pushed David's t-shirt up over his head and leaned her head on his naked chest. She could hear his heart beating, and wondered if he could hear hers because it was hammering inside her chest. She ran her fingers across the scar on his chest. She would never understand what Alice did, and shuddered.

'It's alright.' His face was still recovering from the injury, and his clothes fit him better. Plastic surgery could make the scars fainter, if and when David was ready.

'I know.'

He tipped her head, so she looked into his eyes, the lamp in the corner providing enough light. Cara pulled his face to hers and kissed him. Gently, so gently, she ran her tongue around his lips, and when he opened his mouth to her, she ran her tongue across the tip of his.

David

David had Brandon wrapped in his arms when he woke the next morning. The blanket had been pulled up around his shoulders to cover them both. He gently extracted his son from his arms and pulled the blanket over him before checking the child in the bunkroom. She was sleeping soundly and tucked tightly into bed.

Birds were singing their early morning song as sunlight filtered through the treetops onto the curtains. He pulled on a Golden State Warriors windbreaker and closed the door behind him. Cara stood on the back porch, his red and blue dressing gown wrapped around her. Her golden curls sparkled in the sunlight that streaked through the treetops as she looked over the valley.

'Morning,' he said as he wrapped his arms around her.

Cara turned in his embrace, 'Have I told you how I love you?' she asked.

'Like I love you.'

'Yes, like you love me.'

He held her in his arms and buried his face in her tangled curls, breathing in before caressing her lips with his. The morning chorus grew louder as a brown and black eagle, its white-tipped feathers catching the morning sun, hovered over the lake, scattering the smaller birds. He tilted Cara's face to show her.

'So free,' she whispered.

'One day,' he said.

'Yes.'

'Daddy,' a little voice called.

David turned to see his son standing at the back door, his hair mussed, his Sesame Street pyjamas scrunched around his middle. Cara tried to pull out of his arms, but he held her close before kneeling to straighten Brandon's clothing.

'Did you have a good sleep?' he asked, lifting his child from the ground.

'Mmm.'

Brandon was taking in the scene before him. It had been a long time since there had been affection in the home David and Alice shared. Brandon would not remember it at all.

'Mimi,' Jennifer said at the back door.

Cara knelt and ran her hands over Jennifer's hair, which was all over the place and sticking out at right angles. She gave up and lifted Jennifer from the ground.

'Where's your daddy? Shall we wake him up?' Cara asked.

Jennifer slid out of Cara's arms. 'Yes.'

Brandon wiggled his way out of David's arms and joined Jennifer as she tiptoed back into the cabin. David took Cara by the hand and followed the children back into the cabin.

Jeremy was grinding coffee, filling the room with an aroma that mingled with the redwood scent of mild spice and sweetness that filled the cabin. He turned and knelt in front of Jennifer, hugging her tightly.

'Where's Toddy?' Jennifer asked.

'Still sleeping.' Jeremy ran his hands through Jennifer's unruly curls. 'Maybe Mimi can fix your pigtails.' He shrugged his shoulders and looked hopefully at Cara. His attempt to restrain Jennifer's curls had failed.

Bacon spitting added to the aroma in the room, and the children chattered as they hurried around the table and put crockery and cutlery out.

'Can we go for a swim?' Jennifer asked.

'When the water's warmer. It's still too cold this early in the morning,' Jeremy told her.

He put the makings of breakfast – coffee, bacon, toast, pancakes, and eggs – on the table. The children banged and crashed chairs as they pulled them towards the table.

'Good morning,' Todd said as he came into the room, rubbing his hands through his blond hair. And because they were in a private home with those they loved, Jeremy took him in his arms and kissed him softly on the lips. 'Morning.'

Jennifer's chair squeaked along the floor as she pushed it back and ran into his arms. He picked her up, and she kissed his face.

David held Cara's hand; he wanted a love he could share too, but he had to be aware of Brandon. Brandon had a mother who wasn't living at home, whom he had visited twice in the last ten days. He was too young to understand why. His son sat on a chair watching Jeremy kiss Todd, and Jennifer scrunched Todd's face. Brandon glanced at David holding Cara's hand.

Affection between adults was not something Brandon saw at home. He saw his grandparents display affection, but it was always restrained in front of the children.

David wanted today to be more than just a weekend. He wanted Brandon to see adults displaying affection as normal, to live in a home filled with love, not what the house they lived in was filled with. He hoped that day would come soon.

He pulled a chair close to Brandon and ruffled his hair before plopping a kiss on his cheek.

Chapter Thirty-six

Cara

On the 21st of July, with just over three weeks left on her visa, Cara received another letter.

She sat with David on the sand at Baker Beach, The Golden Gate Bridge gleaming tall and strong, its towers reaching for the wispy clouds that flew by in a pale blue sky. Todd had exhausted every avenue to get her an extension on her visa. The Department of Immigration was unyielding. Cara would go back to Perth on the 14th of August.

The summer sunshine reflected off the paper in Cara's hands, and she took the words in.

> *My dear Cara,*
>
> *I wish to let you know the DNA test results have arrived in Ireland. I have hit a wall with the church over this issue. There seems to be no bending of rules, and I have been told that under no circumstances will there be a DNA test done on Rose. I am sorry to put you through all that for nothing.*
>
> *I am sure Rose is your mother, and I have included with this letter a golden locket that belonged to her. The stone wall I met with my enquiries at High Park crumbled a little, and I have reliable information about a young postulant who came to High Park from an orphanage.*

This young woman was abandoned at birth in 1942. She had no personal possessions apart from this golden locket found with her as a baby. Her name was Teresa Rose Maloney, as asked for in the note left with her. In her Novice year, she took the name of Margaret Rose. She went to teach in a school in Perth, Western Australia but returned to High Park in 1964 and stayed there until she passed away in 1966.

I hope this information will bring you comfort. Remember, your mother loved you and would want a happy life for you.

God Bless and keep you safe,

Briget

Cara opened the small package and turned a heart-shaped golden locket over in her hands. There was no inscription on the back. The latch opened to her fumbling fingers and revealed a faded picture of a young man in uniform.

My grandfather.

Cara closed the locket and handed it to David. He placed it around her neck, closed the catch, and wrapped her in his arms.

Chapter Thirty-Seven

Cara

A week later, Cara answered a knock on the door. Her stomach lurched as she looked around. Alice stood before her, her blonde hair swinging in a pigtail, Brandon beside her.

'Hello Cara,' Alice said. 'Brandon has pictures he wants to show to sweet Cara. May we come in?'

Alice is in the clinic. Why is she on the doorstep? Why does she have Brandon with her? Cara stepped back as Alice jostled her way through the door. She shouldn't have done that; she should have slammed the door shut, but Brandon was looking up at her.

'Can we have some coffee together? I have my car, we could go for a drive,' Alice suggested.

'I don't think that's a good idea.' Cara backed into the living room.

'Brandon, show sweet Cara your pictures.'

Cara took an A5 envelope from the little boy's unsteady hand.

'Brandon would like some juice, Cara, wouldn't you, Brandon?'

Brandon looked from his mother to Cara. 'Enifer... home?'

'No, sweetheart,' Cara said. Jennifer was at a pre-school dance program to fill in the empty days of the school holidays.

'Would you like to play with her toys?'

Brandon nodded.

'You know where they are.'

Brandon scampered into the bedroom.

Cara clutched the envelope in her hands, trying to think. She turned to face Alice. 'What do you want?'

'You haven't seen your pictures.' Alice snatched the envelope from Cara's hand, marched across the room, and sat at the table. 'Come and see them.'

Cara hesitated before moving slowly across the room. Alice ripped open the envelope and laid the photos on the table. 'Such beautiful pictures. I'm sure all the courts and newspapers would love to see them.'

Cara's heart broke when she saw the pictures. The precious moments she'd spent with David. The first day on Baker Beach, lunch at Fisherman's Wharf. David going in her front door, kissing him goodbye later at that door. Sharing an ice cream, holding hands in the park. A stolen kiss on a windblown hill, a precious moment on the beach only last week.

'Now, what are we going to do about this?' Alice asked.

Cara's phone was in her bag which was hanging on the back of a kitchen chair. She reached for it. Needing it.

Alice jumped from her chair and grabbed Cara's wrist, causing her to wince. 'We don't want to make a fuss … don't want to upset Brandon, do we? I think you should come for coffee.'

'Brandon,' she called. 'Come along, we are going for coffee with Cara.'

Brandon came out of the bedroom clutching Jennifer's Elmo doll. 'Can Elmo come?'

'Yes,' Cara said.

***

Cara didn't know her way around San Francisco that well – she'd been a visitor for a few months – but she did recognise the Presidio Children's playground. She'd been there on several occasions with Jennifer.

Alice parked the Lexus on the sloping street beside an old Victorian house and said, 'Come along, Cara. David is waiting for you.'

Possibility floated in the gentle breeze surrounding Cara as she stepped out of the car.

'Brandon, Daddy is waiting for you,' Alice said. She helped the little boy from the back seat of the car.

'Daddy is here?' Brandon asked.

'Daddy is waiting for us; he is in the playground.' Alice held Brandon's hand as they crossed the street, then let him run past the tennis courts along the pathway to the children's playground. Cara hurried behind him, but Alice grabbed her arm and stopped her. 'He knows his way; you don't need to worry about him.'

'Daddy's not here,' Brandon said. He peered through the metal fence, and climbed on the playground's railing.

'Daddy must be late; he will be here soon.' Alice opened the gate and sat Brandon on a bench under a bush. 'You must wait here for him; you can play with the other children until he gets here.'

'Will Cara stay?'

'No, she has to help Mummy.'

Brandon clutched the red Elmo doll to his chest, and Alice turned to leave. 'Mummy,' Brandon whimpered.

Cara saw a glimmer of concern in her eyes as Alice turned and looked at her child alone on the park bench. Cara tugged her arm free of Alice's grip. 'I should stay with Brandon.'

'No.'

There seemed to be an out-of-school group on the playground. *I can call out and attract attention if need be.* 'You can't leave him here on his own.'

The concern disappeared from Alice's face, replaced with the hatred Cara had seen in Austria. Cara stumbled, her legs not wanting to work – she couldn't leave Brandon. Alice wrenched her arm, pulling her away. 'Don't make a fuss, Cara. You don't want to upset Brandon. David should be here.'

Would someone notice a little boy alone? David must be on his way; Alice wouldn't leave Brandon alone if David weren't on his way. But Cara knew David would never have agreed to that; he would never have agreed to let Brandon wait on his own.

David

David abandoned the taxi when it got stuck in traffic and ran the last mile home. His leather work shoes weren't meant for running, his feet told him, and his light blue shirt stuck to his body. He ran up the steps of his home, but a police officer at his front door stopped him.

'Hey, you can't go in there,' she said.

'He's my son.'

She stepped aside to allow David into the foyer. He took deep, calming breaths and forced himself to walk. His little boy was sitting on his grandmother's knee at the dining table.

'Daddy.' Brandon called and ran into his arms. 'Mummy said ....' He heaved a sob, and tears fell. He clutched a dirty red Elmo doll.

'I'm here.' David carried the weeping child back to the table and sat on a chair. His house was full of strangers in uniform. David looked up as a burly detective entered the dining room. 'Detective Nugent, I would not think a missing child required your attention.'

'Maybe not, but your wife and Cara Maloney are missing, and there are some questions about Cara Maloney's involvement in the attempt on your life.'

Is it time to tell the truth?

'Miss Maloney was not involved in that,' David said.

'I need to talk to you alone.' The detective's eyes probed David.

Brandon huddled in his father's arms, away from the strangers in his home. David put Brandon in Jessica's arms and followed the detective into the sitting room.

David knew his face was pale when he returned to the dining room. He lifted Brandon from Jessica and held him tight as he looked into his mother's eyes. Swallowing a deep breath, he wiped his cheeks. There were no words to tell his parents that news.

Peter Nugent stood beside the dining table and said, 'The Lexus was parked at the cabin, but it's not there anymore.' He didn't go into any further details as David had asked.

'Detective Nugent, you need to find my wife, and I need to look after my son, you know where we are if you require any further information,' David said.

'I will show you out,' Robert Hayle said.

'We will be in touch if we have any news.'

David nodded.

He needed to look after his son. Cara would want that. Running his hands through the little boy's hair, and up and down his body, checking for injuries, he wiped the tearstains from his face and held him tight on his knee. 'I'm here; it's okay now, I'm here.'

'Luckily, he knows his name, bits of his address, and family details,' Robert said as he closed the front door and shut the world out.

'What happened? Where is mummy?' David coaxed gently.

Brandon sniffed and looked up at David. 'She went with Cara. She said you will come to the park for me. I had to wait, Daddy.'

'I'm sorry I wasn't there straight away. Can you tell me what happened?'

'A nice lady with a doggy asked my name. She gave me a drink, and she had some candy.'

All the things we say not to do.

David looked at his mother.

'He was found at Presidio Playground. A woman walking her dog saw him and thought he was with the other children, but on her way home, she saw him alone and called the police.'

'The police brought me to Nannie and Poppa. The lady's doggy was Maxy … he was nice.'

'I'm glad you like Maxy,' David said.

Brandon knew Nannie and Poppa owned a big shop where Daddy worked. *Where daddy worked with his phone switched off, and his secretary told not to disturb him until he finished what he was working on while his little boy sat crying alone on a park bench.* He turned his phone on to talk to Brandon to find out how his day at out-of-school care had gone, and there were so many missed calls.

Nancy said Brandon was not at the centre, she'd been told his mother picked him up earlier today.

Jeremy said, Cara hadn't picked Jennifer up from her dancing lessons.

Alice was still at the Clinic when he called her father, but when he called the Clinic, Alice was not there. *She was not a prisoner and could not be made to stay against her will.*

David's eyes blurred. *When had the business become so important? What was he doing?*

Nancy stood unsure at the dining room doorway, her eyes red and swollen. 'Shall I make a bath for Brandon, Mr Hayle? I'm sorry.'

He had employed Nancy through a veteran's support program that his great-grandmother had helped fund. Nancy had served in Vietnam as a Nurse, like his uncle. He'd been unsure. Nancy had lost her job and become homeless. His uncle referred her to him, so he'd given her the position to earn a wage, pay her rent, and regain her dignity. Brandon seemed to stitch a tear in Nancy's heart, and they'd developed a bond almost immediately.

'It's not your fault, Nancy, you didn't do anything wrong,' David said. He sat Brandon on the seat, stood, and pulled Nancy into his arms. 'It's not your fault.'

David turned to Brandon and said, 'Nancy will give you a bath. Is that okay?'

'Can Elmo come?'

'Yes.'

***

David stood on the balcony, staring over the rooftops and across the bay. Shadows grew longer. Light bounced off windows as the sky turned orange, and the day began to cool. He could hear voices and clutter in the kitchen below, and when the sliding door opened, he turned to see his grandfather standing there.

'Okay?'

'Yes,' David replied.

But he wasn't. He tried hiding his tears as his grandfather wrapped his arms around him. For a moment, David was a 6-year-old boy who'd fallen off his skis, and for a moment, he let himself be that boy. Then he pulled out of his grandfather's arms, and they sat opposite each other, looking at the pictures on the coffee table.

All his precious moments with Cara, all this time Alice had been watching them, from their first outing at Baker Beach.

'How could she do that to Brandon? How could she hate me that much?' David asked. He felt like someone had cut open his chest and ripped his heart out. How could Alice abandon their son, her son? Her desire to control him must have taken a darker turn to do that to Brandon.

'It's not hatred, it's possession – she wants to control you, you know that.'

Yes, David knew that.

He should have taken Brandon and left the first time he'd come home and found him crying and Alice asleep on the couch

– the first time she'd hit him. But how could he explain his actions? What could he say? Who would have believed him? Alice was the perfect mother; everyone said so.

He looked into his grandfather's eyes and understood; his grandfather knew the truth. David's efforts to hide it had not succeeded; maybe they had not succeeded with anyone. He should have known, why hadn't he?

'Why didn't I see, Grandad?'

'You tried to keep your family together.'

'Yes. I was stupid.' *I was stupid!*

'Not stupid, just doing the best you could. Nothing shameful about that.'

'Brandon's her son. She should love him.'

If she loved him, how could she do that to him?

'She does in her way, but she will use him against you to get what she wants.'

David shuddered. He thought he was making a family with Alice after Brandon was born. He pushed Cara away, to forget, not to think of, and he thought he'd done that, but sometimes she slipped into his mind.

He always felt guilty about that until the day he found out Alice had lied to him about her first pregnancy. That was also the day he found out Alice had not forgotten Cara.

What was Alice doing?

How would this get her control over him? How far would she go?

'What can I do?'

'Where would Alice go – can you think?'

And David knew where Alice would take Cara. A special place he'd shared with Cara, a special memory for Alice to control … in the pictures on the coffee table that Jeremy had bought earlier that evening.

Chapter Thirty-eight

Cara

Alice scoffed at Cara as she tried to open the door of the Lexus as it drove slowly along a winding forest road. 'Don't be silly, Cara. You don't want to get lost out here – there are bears and bobcats in the woods.'

She parked the car and dragged Cara into the family cabin, the cabin that held memories of a time with David and Brandon. *Brandon … is he safe? How long did it take David to reach him?*

'We will stop here for a while; you've been here before, haven't you?' Alice forced Cara up the steps.

Cara looked around, trying to remember where the neighbours lived. Alice pushed her onto a kitchen chair and sat opposite her, she leaned forward and spoke softly.

'David is mine. Why do you keep trying to take him away?' The hate Cara had seen in Austria had not diminished; it was boiling, surfacing, and threatening. 'You can't keep upsetting David like this.'

She looked around the room, pulling her ponytail, shook her head, and muttered, 'You will be gone soon – David is mine.'

Cara froze, and at that moment, she understood the danger she was in. She pushed away from the table. 'He's not yours, you don't own him, he doesn't belong to anyone.'

'Oh, you have some backbone,' Alice smirked. She grabbed Cara by the arm and dragged her across the room to the kitchen area. 'Let's see how he likes pretty Cara after this.' Alice wrenched a drawer open and grabbed a long, silver, black-handled knife.

Cara looked out the window of the Lexus as they drove through tall forest trees with sunbeams flashing across the road. She was hungry, tired, and desperate. Running her hands through her hair, she sucked in air, trying to understand what was happening.

Alice had shoved the kitchen knife at her face, and Cara reacted, knowing she should do something to defend herself. She squirmed and writhed, and tried to pull away, as Alice slashed the knife in her direction. It all seemed so unreal, but then Alice grabbed a handful of her hair and hacked into it, leaving a trail of golden curls on the cabin floor.

Sunset came early in the forest, but there was still light in the day as the Lexus pulled out from the canopy onto a mountain road. Cara knew where she was. The Golden Gate Bridge shone before her, its towers soaring into an orange and pink sky. Sunlight created golden pathways along the darkening water.

'It's hot,' Alice said. 'We should go for a swim. Isn't that what friends do?'

'I'm not your friend.'

'But you are David's friend.'

Alice parked the car. There were no other vehicles in the carpark, so she walked around and opened Cara's door.

'Now don't think you can do anything silly,' she said, and opened her bag to show Cara the contents.

Cara stared at a menacing black object. She'd never seen a gun before, but she knew it was real.

'Come now.' Alice linked her arm through Cara's and forced her away from the Lexus, and down the sandy track to the beach.

Waves crashed on the shore, sucking sand and water back into the ocean. Cara knew enough of beach safety; the rip would carry anyone caught in it out into the bay.

'Let's sit and watch the water,' Cara said.

'That's a good idea. We can wait for David here,' Alice said. 'He will be here soon, your *knight in shining armour.*'

Cara could hope that might happen, but would David know where they were? Was he still looking for Brandon?

The day's sunset in The Bay was magical. The sky turned pink and yellow with tinges of gold as the sun began to slip towards the horizon. Pink, almost red, sand ran down to the water. Cara saw the beauty, and she saw the terror as the ocean dragged sand under and away.

'Let's sit,' Cara repeated. Alice flopped onto the sand and pulled Cara down beside her. 'It's been a long day,' Alice said. 'You must be tired.'

'Yes,' Cara answered before she realised.

She was tired and nauseous, her stomach rolling. She couldn't get the image of a little boy clutching a red Elmo Doll, sitting alone on a park bench, out of her mind.

When she looked at the person beside her, the person who had said kind words, she saw no kindness in the face. Loose strands of hair blew around Alice's face, the band on her ponytail had slipped, and her makeup had smudged. Her hands shook as she wrung them together and scraped her fingernails across her palms.

'How could you do that to Brandon?' Cara asked.

'What?'

'Leave him alone like that.'

'David should have been there; it's not my fault if he's late.'

'David would never do that. He would never leave Brandon alone like that.'

'Oh, you know him so well, do you?'

Alice opened her bag and pulled a container out; she stuffed a handful of pills into her mouth and took a swig from her water bottle. Cara pushed herself away to stand, but Alice grabbed her arm and said, 'Where are you going? Come on, it's time for a swim.'

Cara could see surfers in the water, and people were fishing about a quarter of a mile down the beach. She could swim that far.

People have been swept away by unexpected waves. Cara heard Jeremy's warning.

Alice shoved herself up from the sand, then tugged Cara up beside her. She was unstable on her feet and leaned into Cara, but her grip was firm. Anyone looking on might have thought it was two friends on the beach after a few drinks.

Alice swung her bag over her arm, then pulled Cara down to the water's edge. 'You go first, I'll mind the bag. You should take your shoes and your clothes off. You don't want them to get wet.'

Cara's shoelaces did not come undone easily, and her fingers wouldn't obey their instructions. She pushed her jeans down and pulled her t-shirt over her head. Any warmth left in the day dissipated as icy water splashed Cara's thighs, and she struggled to stay upright in the surf.

I can swim. I can swim.

'Go on. I will be waiting for you when you come out.'

'Alice.'

A voice in the distance.

The world around Cara stopped. The sun hovering on the horizon in a multi-coloured haze of pink and gold – a voice in the distance she recognised.

'Alice.'

That voice again.

'David, there you are. I wondered how long it would take you to find us?' Alice said. 'Look, Cara, it's David coming to rescue you, like he promised all those years ago, and Jeremy, he can't go anywhere without Jeremy.'

Cara didn't dare turn her back on the surf, but she turned side onto the waves to see David racing along the beach while Jeremy used his phone.

'Tell them to stay away.' Alice pulled the weapon from her bag.

Cara held up her hand. 'Don't,' she called, hoping he heard her above the waves and traffic on the bridge.

The colours of sunset began to fade. David stood on the sand, close enough for Cara to see fear in his eyes.

'Brandon?' she whispered.

Okay, David nodded.

'Alice,' David said.

Cara could see him struggle to control his fear. With tears in his eyes and a clenched jaw, he moved a step closer to Alice.

'Now, David, don't be silly,' Alice said. 'Remember, you are mine, not hers.'

'Yes, Alice, that's right, I'm yours, not hers.' David took another step closer, putting himself between her and Alice. Cara saw him remember the last time Alice had pointed a gun at him, but he kept his back straight and his hands still. 'Let Cara go.'

'Brandon?' Alice asked. 'Did you find Brandon?'

'Yes, I'm sorry I was late, but he was okay. Come home to him now?' David held his hand out to Alice.

'You were late, it's not my fault if you are late.'

'Yes, I was late.'

Cara saw vehicles pulling to a stop in the carpark; she saw Jeremy running along the beach. Waves pushed and pulled at her legs. Digging her feet into the sand, she stayed upright as the sky became darker.

'Let Cara go,' David said.

'You're mine,' Alice said.

'Yes.'

'You have to come with me – stay with me.'

'I'll come with you. Let Cara go.' David stepped towards Alice. She shoved the gun into his chest.

The last of the day's light showed her eyes darting around and her lips twitching.

'No ….' Cara whispered. Her chest heaved, and she sucked in air. 'No.'

Cara stumbled, incoming waves burrowing sand away from her feet. Pushing her wet hair away from her eyes, she shoved her feet deeper to regain her balance.

David reached towards her.

'No, David, you are mine,' Alice threatened as she waved the gun at the ocean.

'Come on now, David. We are going for a walk. I'm sure Cara can swim; she will be fine.' Alice linked her arm through David's, tugging him away from the water's edge along the darkening sand.

A fairground of twinkling lights on the bridge reflected off the ocean. David and Alice walked away from Cara, *arm in arm like lovers*. Her numb legs would no longer hold her. The sand-filled rip snaked around her legs, pulling her feet from under her. She heard Alice say, 'You're mine,' as the next wave rolled over her head.

Chapter Thirty-nine

David

Alice slung her handbag over her left arm, the gun tucked away out of sight. There was no one else on the beach, no one to help Cara until Jeremy reached her.

'Don't fret, David, the *little slut* can swim,' Alice said.

David wrenched his arm away from her. There was enough light from the bridge to see Alice, but he could no longer see Cara. He'd walked with Alice to distance her from Cara, but stopped as they approached the rocky black outcrop. He would not continue this farce with Alice.

'Come on, David. 'Alice tugged at his arm. 'Remember when we were younger, when we promised we would never let anyone tear us apart? Remember that day under the bridge, we said we would jump off if anyone tried? You must keep your promise now.'

David shuddered. He remembered that day. They were teenagers and had just seen Romeo and Juliet at the school theatre. Alice was gushing about the love match. He'd been a fourteen-year-old boy wanting to get home to play basketball with his buddies. They'd stood under the bridge, traffic rumbling overhead, and Alice had leaned over, kissed his lips, and said, 'We'll be Romeo and Juliet.'

He'd thought it funny, and never understood why his mother reacted so badly when he told her. She'd insisted he no longer spent time alone with Alice and had tried to keep them apart. That was impossible as the families were woven together over time and business. He had been too young to understand.

'Come on, David.' Alice grew agitated as she pulled the gun from her bag. 'You are mine; you have always been mine, and you must keep your promise.'

'Will you shoot me again?'

'That was an accident. You have to keep your promise now. She can't have you – she's gone now. She can't upset you anymore. It's time to keep your promise.'

'What about Brandon?'

'He's little. He will forget you.'

David's blood turned to ice. Her smile, reflected in the light, showed him what he couldn't believe, what he should have known.

Alice had always been a spoilt child, and maybe she never grew up. She placed the blame for her actions elsewhere and took no responsibility for them. She believed she could have whatever she wanted. And if anything stood in her way, she would lie and deceive to get what she wanted, like she had done when she'd told him she was pregnant.

And now he understood. Alice would destroy him if she could not control him. She had dictated and manipulated, but David never thought she would go this far. He never thought she would treat Brandon or use him like she had. That was a step further than David thought possible. He shuddered in the cold, as waves pounded the black rocks, spraying on his face and clothing.

Alice scrambled onto the rocks, slipping and stumbling in her high heels. He could have laughed at the scene before him, but Alice waved the gun at him and flung her bag onto the rocks.

'Come on, David,' she said.

David clambered over the outcrop. A rolling wave swept over the rocks, water rushing around his ankles. Alice grabbed her bag and reached out, expecting him to take her hand and walk with her. He stood still, light from the bridge casting shadows on the darkening rocks. He could hear waves crashing. Alice moved to higher ground, reflected light shining on the gun she pointed at him.

The next wave hit him, pulled his feet out from under him, and dragged him over the rocks. He heard the gun explode.

The ocean roared, sucking and spitting, slamming David onto the rocks. He felt warmth in the chilled water as his blood flowed around him. He struggled to keep his head above the water as it thundered over the rocks.

He heard Alice cry out as the ocean pulled her under.

Cara

Cara could swim and kept herself afloat by remembering her swimming lessons from school. *Let the water take you, don't struggle against it, swim across it, and then back to the shore.* But the water at Cottesloe had never been this cold. She couldn't swim back to the shore. Her strength had gone when a stranger on a surfboard pulled her from the ocean. He helped her ashore and into Jeremy's arms. Jeremy wrapped his shirt around her.

Cara's knees buckled. She was so cold she had stopped shivering and needed to sleep. Jeremy kept her awake, tapping her cheeks and patting her arms and legs until she began to shiver and tremble.

'David,' Cara cried. 'Alice ….'

'I know.'

'We have to find him.'

'We will.'

Jeremy took the blanket from the paramedic, who'd run up beside them, and wrapped it tightly around Cara.

'Is there anyone else out there?' the paramedic asked.

'David. She took David. She has a gun.' Cara's teeth chattered.

The paramedic handed Jeremy a flask, and Cara sipped the drink, her hands too cold to grip.

In the quiet between waves, a car backfired, it might have been a car backfiring, but Cara knew it was not.

'David.'

'We will find him,' Jeremy said.

By now, the beach was crowded. The Paramedic, joined by his crew mate and several police officers, had gathered around.

'Miss Maloney?' Cara looked into the face of Peter Nugent.

'You have to find David; she went that way.'

Cara waved her arm toward the Golden Gate Bridge, surprised by how far up the beach she was. She could see the black rocks outlined by the light from the bridge.

'In the water, someone's in the water,' a voice called.

Cara heard the words, words of hope. She stumbled to her feet, leaning on Jeremy.

'Where?' Cara scanned the ocean.

Black sky, the light from the bridge creating golden splashes in the dark ocean, Cara couldn't see anything.

A light shone. A spotlight on swimmers in the water. Two swimmers, one supporting the other – David helping Alice, both struggling with their survival. Cara saw the next wave pull them under.

Divers in wet suits, who, unbeknown to Cara, had arrived, ran into the water carrying rescue devices.

One swimmer was carried ashore and placed on the sand, while the other was still in the ocean. Cara could not see who was on the beach in the shadows, but then the spotlight showed her, the swimmer, receiving CPR.

Cara shoved out of Jeremy's arms and tried to run, but her legs would not work. She fell to her knees, trying to breathe and move. Forcing herself upright, she forced her legs to work, staggering down to the water's edge, finally running as she reached the water. Jeremy grabbed her, pulling her away from the rolling ocean. She pushed him away, pounding his chest, but he held her tight.

'No, Cara.'

'David's out there … in the …..'

'You can't help him … let the divers.'

Cara's eyes scanned the ocean … nothing.

***

Cara saw divers coming ashore, a limp body between them. Somebody coughed and spluttered, a head lifted, and the supporting arms were shoved away.

David lurched across the sand. He glanced at the paramedics on the beach before he fell to his knees where Cara stood. Jeremy released his hold on her, and she dropped to her knees on the sand in front of David. She could see dark blotches on David's clothing; she could feel Jeremy hovering behind her, and knew he wasn't alone.

'I'm sorry.' David reached out, but she pulled away from his touch, waving her hands around in front of her, shuddering, her chest heaving, her words incoherent.

'It costs too much, David. Too much for us to love each other. Alice would rather you dead than let you be with me.' She looked over David's shoulder at the blonde hair of the woman the paramedics used a defibrillator on.

Further along the beach, she saw Mother Superior. *Why is she here?* She heard those words again: *No one could or would ever love you.*

'Don't, Cara, please don't.' David grabbed her hands, held them tight, and pulled them to his lips. They were warm. How could he feel warm after being in the water all that time?

Like spilt treacle, a dark shadow spread across the sand he knelt on. Pain etched his face, and he sucked in air, choking.

'I can't, David. I can't lose you. How will I live if she kills you?' Cara mumbled.

Would Alice finally tear them apart? Could she let him choose to love her? Was their love worth his life?

'She won't. I love you,' he spluttered, then he choked out. 'How will I live if you are not in my life?'

Cara couldn't breathe. Their love had been worth waiting for, he would not let Alice tear them apart. She swallowed her fears.

Wild lilies and sun-splashed mud filled her mind. She leaned her forehead against his and whispered. 'I love you.'

Mother Superior disappeared, and there was only Alice on the beach.

'Hey, buddy, take it easy.' A paramedic stood beside them. David was helped into a sitting position, his blood-stained jeans cut away, and the gash down the side of his shin exposed.

'Alice?' David asked.

'Being looked after … we need to take care of you.'

Sand blew into Cara's face as she sat beside him. The night sky filled with light, and a helicopter's blades whacked the air as it landed. Cara watched Paramedics lift Alice onto a stretcher and place her in the helicopter.

'We need to get you to the hospital,' the paramedic told David.

'No. I need to go home, my little boy.' David tried to push himself from the sand, but his leg would not support him, and he collapsed into the arms of the paramedic.

David was helped onto a stretcher that had been placed beside him, and an injection was pushed into his thigh.

'You need to be checked out as well, miss.'

'I'm okay,' Cara wheezed, but she stumbled, and her legs crumpled when she tried to stand. The blanket keeping her warm dropped to the sand. Jeremy felt like he was on fire when he put his arms around her.

***

The Emergency department was noisy and full of injured and sick people, people needing help and those trying to get help for them. Drunks and drug addicts demanded attention, victims of crime, police trying to help. Cara wondered where she fitted.

David was in a cubicle behind a blue curtain, and she was wrapped in a blanket, sitting in a comfortable chair, with warm drinks and a hot water bottle. Her temperature was checked every fifteen minutes, and she was beginning to feel warm. David's eyes were closed, kept that way by the morphine injections in his thigh. His leg was not broken, but he needed surgery. Could she sign the consent form?

Cara looked up as the curtain around the cubical peeled back, and a little blond head peered around the corner.

'Daddy?' Brandon said.

'He's sleeping.'

'Mummy?'

'She is asleep too.'

His chin quivered, and he screwed a fist into his red eyes and clutched the red Elmo doll to his chest. Cara held her arms out. 'Would you like to sit with me next to Daddy?'

Brandon nodded and crept forward, his eyes blinking, barely open. Cara helped him onto her knee, and his eyes closed as she pulled the blanket around him and Elmo. She kissed his blond hair and said, 'Goodnight, little one.'

'Night, Mimi.' Brandon's muffled words overcame her. He'd heard Jennifer call her by that special name often enough to understand what it meant.

Cara held the little boy close to her heart. The day engulfed her. The clock on the wall told her it was tomorrow, and tears ran down her cheeks as she looked across the cubicle to Jessica and Robert.

Chapter Forty

Cara

Cara's visa to stay in the USA expired on August 14, 1993, but she was allowed a two-week extension as the police investigated the night on the beach.

There were so many questions, but what could she say? Why had Alice left Brandon alone on the bench in the park? Where was David? Was David aware that Alice had left the Clinic? Had Alice fallen or been pushed into the ocean? Why was David in the ocean? What was Cara doing that day with Alice? How could she let her leave Brandon alone in the park?

Cara was the only witness to Alice leaving Brandon alone, David would never have agreed to that, and Cara would never have agreed to that. Alice had a gun; she'd forced Cara into the ocean. No, Cara hadn't seen what had happened once David walked away with Alice. Yes, she was on the beach when Alice was helped ashore, David was still in the water. Too many questions!

She couldn't spend time with David – it would be inappropriate – but she spent time with Jessica and Robert. David would visit, and they would sit on the back veranda overlooking the boats in the harbour and talk, or not.

Brandon and Jennifer would run and play on the lawn that led down to the water while Elmo sat on the bottom step watching.

Eventually, the questions stopped. The children returned to school, and Cara's extended visa expired.

***

On the 1st day of September 1993, Cara left her heart in San Francisco, unaware there was an old song saying just that. The little ones she held and could not show her tears, then Jeremy and Todd, who she knew were making a wonderful home for Jennifer, then Jessica and Robert, who had made the last weeks tolerable. And David.

She left David in San Francisco.

The flight from San Francisco to Perth took over thirty-five hours, with stopovers in Los Angeles and Sydney. Cara thought she would never get home. She splashed out and took a taxi home from the airport.

The traffic on Great Eastern Highway was the same, cars rushed up and down, horns beeped, and roadworks slowed the flow. The Causeway over the Swan River from Victoria Park and the drive along Riverside Drive still stopped and started.

Eucalyptus filled the air, and Cara sucked it in, but in September, with spring in the air, yellow wattle tickled her nose and made her sneeze. Cara paid the taxi driver and stood under a cloudless cerulean sky. She gazed across the green lawn to the river flowing past as a gentle morning breeze tugged at the loose strands of her hair.

Cara dragged her cases up the stairs to the first floor –the lift was out of order, again. She put the key in the lock, pushed the door open, and pulled it shut behind her. She'd been brave for what seemed an eternity, and now, alone in her own home, she didn't have to be.

Cara left her bags on the floor where they fell, stumbled to the bathroom, stripped her dirty, travel-weary clothing, turned the shower to hot, waited for the water to heat and stepped over the hob. The warm water flooding around her body did nothing to ease the pain in her heart. She slid down to the shower floor, tucked her arms around her knees and sobbed.

She slept for days, it seemed, and when she woke, the lights in the buildings across the river twinkled, and the new moon allowed stars to sprinkle the dark sky. She made coffee and sat on the balcony, grateful to Liz and Mike for filling her pantry and fridge. A cold spring wind blew across the river, and Cara pulled a Golden State Warriors windcheater over her head, drawing in David's scent. She closed her eyes, and he was there with his arms around her, the trauma of the past months hanging in the air.

Cara looked at the stars. The Southern Cross hung low in the sky, the pointer stars touching the horizon. Lights shone across the river; traffic rolled along Riverside Drive, and a jet airliner crossed the sky. She breathed deeply and let herself sink into David's arms.

***

On the 12th of September, in a church on Shepperton Road, Victoria Park, where candles burned, the twelve stations of the cross sat on the walls, and a man hung on a cross behind the altar, Cara stood beside the baptismal font.

She was to promise to support the religious upbringing of Liz and Mike's baby boy so he would live a good Christian life, whatever that meant. Cara had suffered much from those living a *good Christian life*. But she promised, with Liz's permission and if needed, to take the role of his parents in this matter, along with Mike's brother who stood beside her as the priest poured water over the baby's forehead.

Cara could not promise to indoctrinate him in the church rules. But she promised to teach him to be a good person who is kind and caring, and if he believed in any god or gods, she pledged to support him in that. She didn't get struck by lightning when she made this promise, so she thanked the kindness of Father Kelly and believed that God, he or she, understood.

Later that evening, after a day of celebrating the child's baptism, Cara waited at home for a phone call. David called if he could. The time difference, San Francisco being fifteen hours behind Perth, made it hard, she was either going to work, or he was, although, at the moment, he wasn't working. He would call before she went to bed. When the phone rang at 7.00 pm, 4.00 am in San Francisco, her hands trembled, and she took deep breaths before picking up the receiver.

Cara placed the receiver back on the wall and wiped her tears away. There had been so many tears and so much cruelty, and until the very end, the cruelty continued.

Briget had said:

> '*I am sorry, the bodies were exhumed, cremated and re-buried on 11th September. There was no public funeral, no time for families to say their goodbyes. I arrived at Glasnevin Cemetery in time to see the urns placed in the grave and the sand filled in. Some family members were able to get to Glasnevin in time to see the burial, but most did not.*
>
> *I am sorry. Any chance the church and the state had to show compassion has been lost. I can only hope that one day the truth will be acknowledged, and some justice for the victims of these laundries will be found.*'

And then there was nothing more to say.

Chapter Forty-one

Cara

Cara bent forward, and ran her hands through a mop of blond hair. Brandon stood mesmerised watching the fish in the tank circle around. Coloured stones lined the floor, and light sliced through the water, creating a blue bubbling cascade. Tropical and edible fish swam in, over and around the ornaments. Lobsters crawled around the tank bottom, their long tentacles tapping the glass sides.

She looked across the crowded restaurant floor to the counter where David stood ordering. He waved to indicate outside or inside. Cara would always go outside, weather permitting, and today it was.

'Shall we go sit with Daddy?' she asked, stretching her back and standing straight.

Brandon looked up at her, then turned back to the fish tank. A large blue fish swam by, followed by several small blue fish.

'Is that the mummy fish?' he asked.

'It might be.'

'Do mummy fishes go to heaven?' Brandon turned his face to hers.

'I think all mummys go to heaven.' Cara caught her breath.

'Like Jennifer's mummy?'

'Yes, like Jennifer's mummy.'

'Like my mummy – she's in heaven too?'

'Yes, your mummy is in heaven too.' Cara lifted the little boy from the ground and held him tight, tears spilling down her cheeks as she carried him outside.

David

David found a table outside under a striped umbrella on the decking, summer in Fremantle being much warmer than in San Francisco; he was glad he'd chosen to wear lightweight chinos and a t-shirt. His Ray-Bans kept the glare out of his eyes. Seagulls squawked, the ocean splashed around the edges of the pier and the wind carried the day's catch in the air. Every fishing port the world over must feel the same.

The gentle breeze blew the hem of Cara's white embossed dress around her knees. He saw the tears on her cheeks as she carried Brandon towards him and, standing, he took Brandon from Cara, and then sat with him curled into his chest.

It had been nearly three months since the funeral. There had been hope after he'd managed to bring Alice to shore. She had seemed to be recovering, but the cold water had damaged too much, and infection had set in. She was placed on life support, and he'd been asked to make the decision.

He'd grieved – Alice had always been part of his life. He'd grieved for that, and he'd grieved for Brandon, for the mother who loved him her way. He'd grieved for Alice, who had always been so beautiful and for whom that had been so important, who lay unresponsive with tubes keeping her alive. And he knew no matter what, Alice would not want to spend her life attached to tubes, and he knew he would not let that happen.

He grieved for her parents, who wanted to keep the machines going. They had a court order, and he did not fight them. He let them have the final say, as he would not make that decision against their wishes.

Her funeral took place in the middle of September, the beginning of Fall when the trees that would lose their leaves had begun to change colour. Her casket was lined in white silk, fitting a princess. Her make-up was perfect, and her blonde hair spread around her shoulders. Angelo had given him a one-off design from the 1993 winter collection, and she looked like Sleeping Beauty. He expected her to open her eyes any minute.

There was much discussion about whether Brandon should see his mother. David had refused to let him see her while she was on life support, with machines keeping her alive, her face covered in breathing apparatus, in a sterile hospital room.

Brandon said goodbye to Alice as she lay in her silk-lined casket in a room painted in pastel colours, in a room full of flowers. She looked like the mother he would remember. David had insisted their viewing be private and on this, he did not budge. Once Brandon had said goodbye, the room could open to those who wished to see Alice.

He'd stood with his son in his arms, looking down at Alice. He thought Brandon too young to understand, but he'd asked, 'Is Mummy asleep?'

David didn't want to lie. He told him. 'Mummy is not sleeping, but she will not be coming home with us anymore.'

Brandon had taken hold of David's face, so he looked into his eyes and asked, 'Where will she go?'

He'd hesitated, unsure, and Brandon asked, 'Will she go to heaven with Jennifer's mummy?'

'Yes – she will go to heaven with Jennifer's mummy.' David's tears spilt onto his son's fingers – Brandon wiped them away.

A gentle tap on the door disturbed them, and he turned to see Nancy. There was a funeral to attend, condolences to accept, and people to comfort. He'd taken a deep breath and asked Brandon. 'Are you ready to say goodbye?'

Brandon nodded. David stood him on the stool beside the casket. 'Goodbye … mum … mummy.'

He'd helped Brandon place a kiss on his mother's cheek, then picked him up and carried him to Nancy. Brandon took the red Elmo doll from Nancy, and she closed the door behind her, leaving him alone with Alice.

His son's faltering words shattered him. How had it come to this? Brandon deserved better. David shuddered. There was no point in questions now; he would ensure Brandon remembered Alice as a mother who loved him. He'd leant forward and kissed her forehead.

**

David looked over the top of his son's blond hair as Cara sat on the chair opposite him, her eyes full of tears. He reached across the table and pushed her red curls away from her face.

'Okay?' he asked.

Cara nodded, rummaging through her bag for her sunglasses. The buzzer went off to tell them their food was ready.

'Would you like to help Daddy?' David asked Brandon.

'Can Elmo come?' Brandon asked.

'Why don't I sit Elmo on a chair to wait for you?' Cara asked.

Brandon thought about that, then he said, 'Okay.'

David gave Brandon the buzzer. As they walked towards the food pickup table, he turned and saw Cara take the ragged Elmo doll from his backpack and hold it close to her heart.

He loved her, had loved her since she hit him over the heart with that snowball, it seemed so long ago. So much had happened, so much she had no control over; he should have known Alice better – could he have done anything differently?

He heard his grandfather's words whispering around his head, *you don't take the blame for someone else's actions.*

Letting his love for Cara wrap around him, he ran his hand across his chest and rested it over his heart. A gentle breeze blew Cara's curls across her face, her tender smile reflectingd the last few months, and he knew it would be alright. It would take time, but he knew it would be alright.

Brandon chattered as he smothered his fish and chips with ketchup. David took the bottle from him, placed it on the bench, and carried the tray back to the table.

Cara had placed Elmo on a chair and had pulled it up to the table, so Brandon pushed a chair close to Elmo and scrambled up onto it. David pulled his chair close to Cara's. They shared food, watching seagulls scrounge for bits, and boats pull into the pier until he said, 'Will you come back to San Francisco?'

Cara shook her head, 'Not yet.'

'Can we stay?'

Cara nodded. 'Please.'

Then she said, 'What about your visa?'

'My mother's Australian.'

Her smile was sunshine breaking through the clouds. 'What will you do?'

'Some interesting things are happening at a place called Margaret River with winemaking at the moment.'

Cara laughed gently. It had been a long time since he'd had laughter in his life. 'Do you know anything about winemaking?'

'Not much, but we can learn. Will you come with me?'

'I would like that.'

'We can raise our children by the sea.'

Cara reached for his hand and placed it on her expanding belly. That was a joy he'd never expected to feel again.

He'd known Cara was pregnant when she left San Francisco. There would never be any secrets between them, but it was not something they could share with all that was happening. He was sure his mother had guessed.

'I have something for you,' he said and reached into his backpack. He took out a small velvet box and opened it. 'It took a long time to repair.'

Cara

David took the locket from the box. Seawater had seeped into it, almost destroying the picture inside. 'The restorer has been able to make out the Insignia on the cap, *HMS Hood*. He told me the ship sunk in the Second World War in May 1941. There were only three survivors – we can try and get more information if you want.'

Once, Cara would have wanted that information, and she still did, but not now. Cara wanted to look forward; it was time to look forward. She couldn't change the past. One day, she would visit her mother's grave and find out about her family, but not now.

'Not now, David. Maybe later. Now, I want to be with you and Brandon. I want to look forward, not backwards.'

He placed the locket around Cara's neck and closed the clasp.

Epilogue

Cara and David stood under a green tree on a patch of ground that held several gravestones at Glasnevin Cemetery, Dublin.

Brandon and his little sister Katie-Rose stood beside the pram where their baby brother slept peacefully.

Cara knelt on the ground in front of a gravestone. There was no way of knowing which grave held her mother. The names on the stones gave some clues, but not enough. Still, those buried would have been someone's mother, daughter, or sister.

David knelt beside her. He put his arm around Cara as she placed flowers on the ground, among others, proof that those buried were not forgotten.

The End

Other books by Bernadette Piper

Tomorrow's Roses
Tomorrow's Promise

About the Author

Bernadette grew up in country Western Australia before moving to Perth, where she attended High School.

She worked as an office assistant for many years before backpacking around Europe in the 70's. Returning to Australia, she raised her family and now has three wonderful grandchildren.

Bernadette lives in Secret Harbour, Western Australia and writes from an Australian perspective. She has published *Tomorrow's Roses*, set in Fremantle during 1944-45 and *Tomorrow's Promise*, set in Cottesloe and locations around the world, during the turmoil of the Vietnam War.

When researching a news article which stated *that of 143 bodies exhumed at a grave site in High Park Dublin, only 75 were identified by name,* A Holiday Promise came to mind.

This article took Bernadette back to her school days, of furtive glances across a classroom and the imagination of young girls. The story evolved into one of sacrifice and secrets, of a search for the truth and a father's love.